Readers Love GREYSON McCOY

Bridging Hope
"I truly enjoyed this short, poignant story of overcoming what life has thrown at you and rising above to succeed and live."

—Love Bytes Reviews

"Pierce and Dalton experiment, take risks, and learn that when you have kids, love alone isn't enough – the kids are the most important thing."

—Rainbow Book Reviews

Bridging Lives
"This was a sweet, gentle story…the book was easy to read and I liked the quiet feelings of coming home it gave me."

—OMG Reads

Mending Bridges
"Both men realize that they must do better so that they don't wind up losing out on something they both want…this was a very sweet story of two men who don't want to lose what they have."

—Paranormal Romance Guild

By GREYSON MCCOY

BRIDGING HEARTS
Bridging Hope
Bridging Lives
Mending Bridges
Bridging the Divide

Published by DREAMSPINNER PRESS
www.dreamspinnerpress.com

Bridging The Divide

GREYSON McCOY

Published by
DREAMSPINNER PRESS

8219 Woodville Hwy #1245
Woodville, FL 32362 USA
www.dreamspinnerpress.com

Bridging the Divide
© 2025 Greyson McCoy

Cover Art
© 2025 Reece Notley
reece@vitaenoir.com
Cover content is for illustrative purposes only and any person depicted on the cover is a model.

Trade Paperback ISBN: 978-1-64108-833-6
Digital ISBN: 978-1-64108-832-9
Trade Paperback published May 2025
v. 1.0

Acknowledgments

Thank you to Jo Bird and Renee Mizar for their editorial help and to César Miguel R. Vega Magallón for his much appreciated cultural guidance and advice. I couldn't do this without you all!

Prologue

I DROVE THE ATV across the freshly harvested side of the wheat field, keen to surprise my boyfriend with lunch and a make-out session. I was almost giddy, knowing how surprised he'd be.

When I pulled up alongside the combine, I kept a safe distance and waited for Donny to spot me. When he did, he slowed the huge machine and stopped.

I climbed up the side of it and crawled into my boyfriend's lap. "I brought you lunch."

"Um," Donny said, "might be too much of an audience."

He nodded his head to the side, and I glanced over to see Ben smirking at us through his truck window. The guy was as straight as an arrow, but since Donny brought me to the farm almost two years ago, he'd been nothing but supportive.

Undeterred, I kissed my man deeply and heard the truck door creak open and then slam shut. "You two need to get a room," Ben hollered as he walked toward us.

I leaned back and yelled, "You're just jealous, Ben."

I crawled off my boyfriend and back down. "I brought sandwiches and chips."

Ben immediately attacked the bag on the passenger seat of the ATV, making me laugh.

"Hey, for goodness' sake, clean your grimy hands first. There's wipes in the bag. You two can be so freaking nasty."

Donny climbed out of the combine and popped me on the ass. "*You* are such a princess."

"So that makes you either an ogre like Shrek or a cursed frog prince who needs a kiss?" I replied, and he smirked as he hauled me in for a deep kiss. "Thy curse is broken, though you'll always be my frog."

Donny chuckled as we all settled around the ATV for lunch. I deliberately wiped my hands before I grabbed a sandwich, which earned an eye roll from both men.

I watched Donny and Ben cut up with one another while we ate. I still couldn't believe the direction my life had taken. All this was a total fluke, thanks to my uncle.

Donny and I graduated together from a university here in Iowa. I took a bad-paying part-time job working for a catering company in Des Moines. Donny was working for a farmer outside of town. After a while, a commute on top of long workdays was too much for Donny, so we relocated from the city to his family's farmstead to help Donny's parents. Even though I was broke and Donny made next to nothing, I didn't want to return to central Oregon.

For the time being and with no full-time job prospects on the horizon, I worked as a house husband/boyfriend. There wasn't much my history degree would do for me career-wise unless I went back to school, which I couldn't afford to do.

Regardless, I knew my gifts lay in the kitchen. Heck, before my paternal grandparents died, my grandmother had put me in charge of meals while she helped manage the cattle with my dad and grandpa.

I still think it's interesting that she knew I fit better in the kitchen than the pastures. I was eleven when Grandpa died and almost thirteen when she did, so I never found out if they'd have accepted my sexuality.

Of course, as strict religious people, even to the point of being teetotalers, I doubt they would've. But they tolerated boys in nontraditional roles and vice versa, with Grandma running cattle while I ran her kitchen being a prime example.

The sound of a contented sigh pulled me from my thoughts. "Thanks for the grub. It hit the spot," Ben said as he stood up and headed back to his truck. "You two get your kissin' done so our boy here can get back to work. Got a lot to get done, and we still have to get through the gulch."

Donny moaned. "I hate the gulch. Tell me again why we keep planting that area?"

"'Cause your dad says money is money."

I understood why it was an issue. The gulch was a bizarre canyon that swept through the Dougherty farmland, and Donny's dad farmed right up to the very edge of it. I wouldn't have worked equipment next to it, and I didn't understand why Donny didn't just refuse. It's not like his dad paid him enough to do dangerous work. It's not like his father paid him much and often didn't pay at all. His parents were the most entitled people I'd ever met, and they just expected him to work for free because they let him live in his grandparents' old farmhouse, which was empty and falling apart when we got here.

I kissed my boyfriend and left before I said something offensive about his parents again. There was no love lost between them and me. Donny's family took advantage of him, but he was loyal to a fault. Of course that was also one of the reasons I loved him so much.

I drove back to the farmhouse and began prepping dinner. Ben would join us like he usually did when they were working the fields together. I liked that, actually. Truth was, I liked my role. I wasn't really a house husband. I thought of myself more as support staff, but I did tend to do all the jobs a traditional farmer's wife would.

That left us uncomfortably poor. But when you're in love, who cares if you have money? Not like I ever had much, being from a farming family. Oregon had been cattle, and now I was in Iowa it was all grain, but a farm was a farm, and if there was money in farming, I'd yet to see it.

My phone rang just as I finished adding the onions to the pot. Seeing it was Uncle Henry, I hit Answer. "Hey, Uncle Henry, to what do I owe the honor?"

"Don't play coy with me, Justin. You know why I'm calling."

"'Cause you love me so much?"

My uncle chuckled. "That I do, although I often wonder why, especially when I have a probate case still on my desk that needs to be put to rest so I can get paid, for goodness' sake."

I sighed and plopped down on a kitchen chair. "Tell me again why you can't just send me the papers and let me sign them here."

"'Cause, as I said last time, you need to come home. Both Jeff and I want to see you."

"So this is about you missing me and not legal papers that need to be signed."

"It's about both," my uncle said, and I could hear the smile in his voice.

"You know I don't want to come back there. The memories…," I admitted, feeling the conversation turn somber as my words trailed off.

"He was a son of a bitch, Justin. You deserved more, but you know there's a lot more to come home to than bad memories. Besides, we wanna meet that strapping midwestern farmer you speak so highly of."

"Oh, trust me, Donny wants to come too, but if I bring him there, I'm sure he's gonna talk me into keeping the land and farming it. I'd rather deal with his parents than go back."

Uncle Henry sighed. "Well, son, like I said, your uncle Jeff and I miss you something awful. And you do gotta get this paperwork signed. I'll overnight it to you if you're sure you won't be coming home."

Just then, movement out the kitchen window caught my eye. Ben's truck was barreling down the road toward the house. "Hey, Uncle Henry, I've gotta go," I said as a knot formed in my gut. "Something's wrong."

AN EMPTY and endless void of darkness overtook me in a way I never knew was possible. At least Donny's parents hadn't forced me away from his grave. I lost track of how long I remained at the cemetery after the service, sitting on the ground next to the fresh mound of dirt, feeling utterly alone and adrift. I hadn't just buried my boyfriend; I'd also buried our future together.

Ben startled me when he placed a hand on my shoulder. If not for him, I'd probably have stayed at the cemetery all night. Without a word he helped me stand and practically carried me to his truck. It was then that Donny's brother Jake, who must've been waiting in his car for me, approached and told me I had a week to vacate the family's property or they'd have me removed by the sheriff.

That would've hurt if my heart wasn't already numb, even if their callousness was expected. What I couldn't process was the loss of the man I'd loved so much. Every hair follicle hurt, every fiber of my being missed him, and I was left with nothing.

Well, not exactly nothing. Donny had taken out a five-hundred-thousand-dollar life insurance policy on himself and me earlier in the year. Why? Well, according to his insurance agent sister, who'd sold us the policy, "You need to protect your loved ones, and you're young and healthy, so it's not that expensive." Donny only got a small allowance for the work he did for his father, so I'd been against it, knowing how tight our budget was. But apparently he'd seen the value in it. Thank goodness.

Margaret, although a wily saleswoman, was the one and only decent member of Donny's family. I trusted her, and so had Donny, so

I told him he should get the policy and we could cancel it after she got her commission. Obviously, Donny never informed me that he hadn't canceled it, not that I could begrudge him for it.

Margaret came over the day after the funeral and reminded me of the policy. "It belongs to you. You're the beneficiary," she said as tears formed in her eyes. "At least my parents can't take that away."

We cried on each other's shoulders, which, to be honest, meant more to me than the money. Tears streamed down my face, thinking about the only man I'd ever loved and how the only constant in my life was losing the people I cherished most.

My life in Iowa died with Donny. I was utterly alone and about to return to a place I'd never thought I'd set foot in again—Wilcox, Oregon.

Manuel López

"¡ANTONIO! LEVÁNTATE, flojo," I said.

"Hey," Antonio replied, "No soy flojo. I just know how to work smart."

"You know how to avoid work, ¿verdad?" I said, tossing the keys to him so he could drive the truck to the pasture.

He met me outside, where I'd gone out to wait for him. When he came around the truck, he smiled and climbed in. My fifteen-year-old nephew was desperate to drive, but both his parents and I agreed it was better for him to learn on back roads and in pastures than main roads.

The heat this year had been so bad we'd been forced to put hay out to supplement the dried grass in the fields for the cattle. My brothers and I were freaking out about it. We'd tripled the herd's size since we purchased the land from the Lancaster family.

Luckily, we could rent land from the estate of our recently deceased neighbor. When the probate attorney—the uncle of the guy who now owned it—approached us to rent, we jumped at the chance.

We pulled into the rented pasture, and I waited until Antonio handed me my keys. I climbed out of the truck and leaned back. As I stretched, I noticed my nephew was about to walk away. Ugh, that kid was so good at avoiding work. "Sobrino, bring the tractor over and pull the bale out. You can set it in the ring, right?" I asked.

Antonio just rolled his eyes, *una costumbre gabacha* I wish he hadn't learned. Had my brothers or I done that to our father or anyone else, we'd have felt the consequences. I ignored my nephew and took his disrespect as a sign of the times.

That reminded me of the conversation I wanted to have with my parents… again. For years I'd been begging them to leave Texas. "¡Su nieto necesita a sus abuelos!" I'd said to them time and time again.

After countless years grazing the desert outside Juarez, my father, who had dual citizenship, in the US and Mexico, bought a house in El Paso, and we moved there when my brothers and I were still teenagers.

I loved growing up in El Paso. It was just the right mix of Mexico and United States to feel comfortable. I never really planned to leave the area, but when the oil market collapsed, sending thousands of workers toward El Paso from the oil fields of West Texas, my brothers and I found ourselves out of work.

Then our luck changed. Mamá's best friend, Marta, married Jimmy Lancaster, a cattle farmer from Oregon, who complained about a lack of reliable help on the farm. Carlos and his wife, María, had a young son. They couldn't afford to be out of work. Martín and I were both still living at home, but I could tell my mom was getting stressed with having two grown, unemployed men living under her small roof.

So when Marta talked Mr. Lancaster into hiring us, we happily accepted the job to live on and operate the farm while he and Marta traveled.

That'd lasted a year before Mr. Lancaster offered to sell us the farm and livestock. The offer was too good to refuse.

Unfortunately, Papá wasn't keen on returning to a cattle farm, although we constantly told him we were in a lush environment with lots of grass and plenty of rain, which was true most years.

"Tío," Antonio called, catching my attention, "there's someone at the old house."

I looked toward the farmhouse, situated in the valley not far from the barn where we were moving the hay for the cattle, and saw a vehicle parked out front.

"Stay here, Antonio," I said, "and if there's trouble, call the sheriff." There were rarely any problems in these parts, but the property owner lived somewhere in the Midwest, and his uncle, the attorney who rented the land to us, had assured me the house was vacant, and my family had agreed to keep an eye on the place.

"Hello!" I yelled as I drew closer and saw a man sitting on the front porch. "You can't be here. This is private property."

The young *gabacho*, maybe early to mid-twenties, rose from the porch swing and said, "I own the place and can do as I please. Who are you?"

That stopped me in my tracks, and I looked him over. "No one said the owner was coming into town." I pulled my phone out and speed-dialed the attorney, Henry Erickson. "I'm calling the owner now. You should go before the sheriff is called."

"Hello," Mr. Erickson answered.

"Hi, Mr. Erickson. This is Manuel López. I have a man on the porch at the property you rented us. He's saying he's the owner."

"Oh, sorry, Manuel. Yes, he's my nephew. I forgot to let you know he's moving back into the house."

"Okay, well, that's fine, then. Thank you for confirming." I hung up and was prepared to eat some crow as I pocketed my phone, but I noticed the man staring at me had remained expressionless.

"I apologize. Your uncle asked us to keep an eye on the house since it was vacant. I thought you might be someone trying to take advantage."

The man sat back down and sighed. "I appreciate that, I guess."

I nodded and turned to leave. "So, Manuel López?" he asked. "You're the one renting my pastureland?"

I figured I should at least try to be civil since I needed to keep relations reasonable. I turned back and approached the porch with my hand outstretched. "Yes, I rent your property with my brothers, Martín and Carlos."

"Nice to meet you," he said as he shook my hand. The brief contact coupled with his adorable crooked smile made my breath hitch. Damn, I had such a thing for cute country boys. "I'd offer you something to drink, but I only just got here. I'm afraid the place is a mess."

I nodded and thanked him. "I need to get back to my nephew anyway. He's fifteen and needs supervision." That was only partly true. The man was in every way my type, but this was not the time or place to flirt with a random man—especially our landlord.

Good terms with him were vital because we needed to use his land for at least a few more months. The dry winter was going to hurt us, and we needed all the grazing land we could get. The extra pastures had already saved us thousands.

Unfortunately, the heat wasn't good for the cattle or the butcher shop we ran in Northport. Grilling season had begun and business would be booming. But because of dry conditions and the fire warnings, though, our shop wasn't doing as well.

I shook my head as I returned to where Antonio was driving the tractor in circles. I swear the boy was going to be the end of me. Not that I didn't understand. I'd been very much the same way when I was young.

I waved at Antonio, and he stopped. "Move the tractor back to the barn, and let's head to town. Your dad needs you to help in the shop."

Antonio groaned. He hated working in the butcher shop, so I tried to bring him with me when I had chores to do on the farm. He was a great help most of the time. I knew his mom was disappointed he didn't want to learn to be a butcher, but his new aunt had filled a void there. Cassie and my brother Martín had gotten married a few months ago, and already she was proving to be a fantastic help running the storefront and learning how to butcher some of the easier cuts of meat.

I was more like my nephew and thanked the good Lord that I wasn't expected to help in the shop. We all had a role to play in our family business, and butchering would never be mine. I'm glad we had an outlet for selling our meat, but I was much happier raising the cattle than ushering them to their demise.

Justin Latham

THE FALL and winter after I lost Donny had been the worst of my life. Even when I came out to my father and he tried to kill me, I wasn't this depressed.

As one season rolled into another and the days grew longer, I noticed what I interpreted as my uncles' frustration with me being at their place all the time. Since my return to Wilcox, I'd taken up residence in my uncles' spare room rather than return to the farmstead. Poor Uncle Jeff had tended to me like an old mother hen, and the truth was I needed it.

I wasn't exactly eager to move, but for the sake of my relationship with my uncles and theirs with each other, I finally convinced myself to move out. I gathered my things the night before and packed them into my ancient Subaru Outback, which I'd bought from one of my college friends before graduation. The next morning I got up, hugged my uncles, and told them I was moving back to the farm.

They both looked concerned, but neither tried to stop me. Hosting houseguests, even one's only nephew, had an expiration date.

"How will you manage out there?" Uncle Henry asked.

"Well, there's plenty to keep me busy if the last time I saw the place is any indication."

Uncle Henry cringed, and from his expression, I could only guess it'd gotten worse. I hadn't lived on the farm since I came out, shortly after I graduated from high school. Feeling like I could take on the world and sick of my abusive father's interference, I told my dad I was gay.

Of course, I'd told the uncles years earlier, and they'd both told me to keep it to myself until I could stand on my own two feet.

Even so, none of us expected Dad's reaction. He had hit me ever since my grandmother had passed away, and he'd stopped pretending he wasn't an alcoholic, but he'd never shot at me before that night.

Had he not been dead drunk, which was unlikely since he was always drunk, he'd have killed me. As it was, I still had nightmares of the bullet buzzing past my ear.

I tore out of the house before Dad could take another shot, and I slept in the abandoned covered bridge near our farm. The following day I ran the ten miles to my uncles' house in town and told them what happened.

I learned later that when my father was arrested, he swore he'd kill me and my uncles. Sheriff Jones told Uncle Richard, who was a sitting judge in Northport at the time, that it might be best if I went away to school for a while until my dad had time to calm down.

Strange how things work out… almost like providence. Uncle Jeff had graduated from a college, now a university, in Iowa, and to appease my uncles, I applied and was accepted. The truth was, I had no intention of going to college anywhere. I never considered myself college material, although I maintained pretty good grades through high school.

Before my dad was released from jail, Uncle Henry and Uncle Jeff drove me to the university to ensure I'd arrive safely. They paid my tuition, and that set me on the path that led to today. I'd ended up right where I started, only now I had a useless degree, a shattered heart, and shitty memories of an abusive father who'd gone to meet his maker.

From the outside, the farmstead didn't look all that different from what I remembered. Uncle Henry had been keeping an eye on the place after Dad passed away, and nothing appeared amiss. Sure, the old house could use a coat of paint and probably other small repairs, but it didn't seem too worse for wear at first glance.

The front porch creaked as a walked up the steps. I paused to take a deep breath, then unlocked the front door and walked into utter devastation. The years in the care of my alcoholic father had left the place in ruins. Luckily, the window air conditioner still worked, but after I turned it on, I saw a dead animal in the corner of the room covered in maggots and had to rush out to keep myself from puking.

I was sitting on the swing, feeling sorry for myself, when I saw a man walking toward the house from the pasture. He called out a greeting, sounding stern, then said I needed to get off private property.

I felt a spark of annoyance at being run off of my own land. It was bad enough I was back here at all, let alone that my worthless father had let the place go to ruin and I would have to fix it. I felt defeated, but something about how the man had approached me also made me angry.

"I own the place and can do as I please," I informed him. "Who are you?"

As soon as the words left my mouth, I felt like an ass for being so short with him. While the man looked at me skeptically and called Uncle Henry to confirm my identity, I took a moment to really look at *him*. Even though it felt like I was betraying my Donny, I couldn't help but notice how attractive the man was.

After the man—Manuel, I learned—hung up, I almost invited him in but remembered the dead animal and the trash scattered around the house. Instead I tried to be as friendly as possible.

When he left, I went around the back, peeked in the shed that was definitely leaning a lot more than it had been when I lived here, and found a wheelbarrow, a pair of work gloves, and the old oil drums my grandfather had collected. If I'd thought ahead, I could've had a dumpster delivered, but there was still no way in hell I was going to sleep a night in that house with all the trash and rotting animal carcasses strewn about. That meant I'd have to fill the old drums and hire someone to haul them off later.

But future me could worry about arranging for disposal. For now, I had a hell of a mess to clean.

Manuel

I DROPPED ANTONIO off at the butcher shop and headed home. Three of our cows looked like they could calve at any moment. We hadn't planned on having calves this late in the season, but the stupid bull from the next farm jumped the fence and mated with three of our prize heifers—the three Antonio had planned to take to the state fair last fall. So, even though we specialized in beautiful registered Red Angus, we had three of our best cows about to give birth to low-quality mixed-breed Polled Hereford.

Mr. Lancaster had taught us to control breeding. Calves born in February and March made the best cows, as their mothers would have fresh grass to graze on before the heat set in. So the best time to get a good price for year-old steers was February through April. Even after we took over for Mr. Lancaster, we continued that routine.

We had wanted to give the heifers another year to come into their own before they gave birth to calves. But lady cows wanted what they wanted. Now we'd have mutt calves.

We'd stuck the expecting moms in the barn by the homestead where our landlord, "Señor Sexy," now lived. The barn was by a stream, which meant the temperature was much easier on the cows than at the barn next to the home my two brothers and their families and I shared.

As I drove back from the shop, I decided it would be best if I got a quick nap in case I needed to stay up while the cows gave birth. As I fell asleep, I was thankful that Antonio was with his parents at the shop, because with him around, there'd be no sleep, no matter how tired I was.

I SLEPT AN hour, which was more than I expected for a siesta. I threw my clothes on and headed back to the barn to check on the cows again.

The first thing I saw as I pulled up was a line of oil drums stacked alongside the house, leading toward the back door. Heading toward the barn, I watched as the owner came down the backdoor ramp pushing a wheelbarrow, then removed the lid of a drum and lifted the wheelbarrow to dump its contents inside.

My first thought was that the guy was working harder than he needed to. I'd done enough demo work to know you didn't want to be lifting anything you didn't have to. But it was none of my business, I reminded myself, and went to check on the heifers. All three seemed fine, each tucked into their stable, chewing away at their cud.

I stepped outside just in time to see the guy lose control of the wheelbarrow and spill the contents onto the ground. Although I knew it was a bad idea, I decided to help.

"Hey, need a hand?" I asked as I pulled my work gloves from my back pocket.

He looked up at me wearing a scowl, frustration etched across his face.

"I need a fucking bulldozer," he said. Then he finished tossing the spilled garbage into the drum.

I bent down to right the wheelbarrow. "Thanks," he said. "I'm about done, at least for now. I'll be okay."

I decided to follow him into his house. I had only been inside the place once when I first met his uncle, Mr. Erickson, to sign the lease paperwork. The attorney had tried to convince us to rent the farmhouse too, but I took one look around and flat-out said no. "Can't say I blame you," he'd replied.

Glancing around I could tell that the guy had done some pretty serious cleaning. It still looked like a cyclone had hit it, but at least he'd made some headway. "You've made progress," I said in admiration of the work he'd done in the stifling heat of the day.

"Well, if I'm gonna live here, I don't have much choice."

I shrugged. "Yeah, if you don't want to live in squalor, at least."

"I don't, but I'm pretty wiped out. I think I'm gonna go rent a hotel room for the night and take a nice long shower." He looked from side to side, apparently taking stock of what remained of the mess, and let out an irritated sigh. "I had no idea the house had gotten this bad."

"Renters?" I asked.

He shook his head and frowned. "No, just an old, worthless alcoholic."

I remembered what Mr. Lancaster had said years ago about this farm and its owner. "He's a raging alcoholic and not a good man. You should stay off his land, and if one of the cows goes over there, you come get me."

I suspected the previous owner had probably been this guy's relative, but I wasn't willing to pry. I had terrific parents—hardworking, loving, and loyal—but my dad's father was rough on him. I immediately felt bad for the guy, and before I knew what was happening, I asked, "Well, I'm happy to help you clean up. When do you plan to start again?"

He stared at me with a curious expression, then asked, "Why would you help me?"

I blushed despite myself. "You look like you need a hand, and your uncle gave us a great deal on leasing your land, so I don't mind. Besides that," I added quickly to lighten the moment, "I have a nephew who could use the hard labor."

He smiled. "People around here like nothing more than seeing a young man work. That's farm life."

I chuckled. There was a lot of truth to that. I'd noticed parents were quick to pawn their teenage boys off on farmers.

"So, what time should we be by in the morning to help?"

"I'm going to try to get here early, maybe five-ish? I'd rather do most of this before the temperatures reach where they are now."

"I agree, so I'll see you tomorrow. Oh, and do you need a dumpster?" I added.

He laughed. "Yeah, using the oil drums isn't ideal, but I doubt we can have one delivered anytime soon."

"Oh, no problem. Pete over at the dump owes me a favor… well, several, if I'm honest. I'll have him drop one off tonight. Can he just put it off to the side of the driveway there?"

The guy stood speechless for a moment and nodded. "Yeah, Mr. López, you're becoming a lifesaver."

"Nah, just being neighborly. I'll see you tomorrow morning."

Justin

THERE WAS something therapeutic about throwing your abusive and neglectful father's shit in the trash. But all that wore off when the temperature turned from barely comfortable to blazing hot.

The house stank—not only of rotten animals but of my unclean father as well. The lingering stench didn't help my souring mood as I filled all eight of the big oil drums. I'd resigned myself to start shoveling shit out the door and onto the ground if I did any more work. Which I was fully prepared to do, considering I wanted to move in as soon as possible.

I only called it a day after the handsome neighbor came to my rescue. As I watched Manuel drive off, images of Donny rushed through my mind, accompanied by an all-too-familiar aching sadness. I plopped down on the porch swing, leaned my head back, and closed my eyes.

I hadn't thought of or even looked at a guy besides my Donny since he swept me off my feet during our freshman year. Well, okay, that's a lie. A handsome man turned heads, mine included, but that didn't mean I had any desire to touch them. Now Donny had been gone a matter of months, and I was already checking out the good-looking guy next door.

It felt dirty, like I was cheating on him, and it nearly sent me back down the spiral of despair. I had almost convinced myself to call my uncle and get Manuel's number in order to turn down his offer to help when I heard a car turning into the driveway.

Uncle Henry and Uncle Jeff got out of the car, came up to the porch, and pulled up a couple of chairs. As they sat in the old, rickety things, I prayed neither ended up on the ground.

"You okay?" Uncle Henry asked.

"Well, no. But I'm not dead either." I meant it as a joke, but my voice held no humor. I felt too wrecked.

They both nodded. "Why did you come here today after all this time?" Uncle Jeff asked, always one to get right to the point.

I shrugged. "It was time, but I wasn't prepared for how bad it was inside."

"If you hadn't just taken off like you did, one of us would've come with you. You don't have to do all this on your own. You know that, right?"

I shrugged again. "I've taken advantage of your hospitality long enough. It's time I stood on my own two feet."

"Bullshit," Uncle Jeff said as he stood up and began to pace. "Listen, Justin, you're as much our kid as you can get. We love you no matter what, but you are as stubborn as your Uncle Henry. Why on earth would you try to tackle this mess by yourself? Is it some self-punishment thing?"

I hadn't thought of it that way. He might be right, but what other choice did I have? I didn't want to overstay my welcome and risk souring the only good relationships I still had in life. "I know you love me, and I appreciate you both so much, but I still saw the relief when I told you I was leaving."

Uncle Jeff stopped pacing and turned to face me. "What you saw, young man, was relief you'd finally decided to face this demon. Our home is yours anytime you need it, and that's the end of that discussion."

I saw Uncle Henry look down to hide his smile. "Now I've had about enough of this," Uncle Jeff continued. "You'll come home tonight. After you get cleaned up, 'cause, son, you smell to high heaven, we'll order a pizza—the one you like with all the meat on it—then sit down as a family and devise a plan."

I met my uncle's gaze and had to resist a smile. Uncle Jeff had gone off on me in a similar way when he whisked me off to college in Iowa and demanded that I let him and Uncle Henry pay my tuition. I'd flat-out refused until Uncle Jeff did exactly what he was doing now.

The man was the definition of meek and humble until you pushed him too far, and then he was anything but. And in those times, like now, he brooked no argument. Uncle Jeff was down the steps and halfway to the car when Uncle Henry stood to leave.

"See you back home," Uncle Henry said under his breath, and I nodded.

"Yeah, guess you will."

When my uncles were gone, I gave in to the torrent of emotions the day had stirred up.

I let the tears flow for all the love and unconditional acceptance my uncles had fiercely given me. Those two men were my foundation. I didn't even know I needed a come-to-Jesus talk from Uncle Jeff, but he always seemed to know what I needed when I needed it.

I let the tears flow for all the loss I'd endured. Not just Donny and my hopes and dreams around that relationship, but also my grandparents. Hell, I even mourned the decent relationship I might've had with my father, had he not been lost to his own addictions, prejudices, and hatred.

Once the tears subsided, I closed up the house without locking it. If I were lucky, somebody would waltz in and claim all the crap before I arrived to clean it out tomorrow.

That reminded me Manuel would be here with his nephew and had arranged for a dumpster to be delivered. My reservations about the man were replaced with determination to get on with it. And right now, ridding the house of the mess my father had created sounded like the best plan.

Manuel was handsome and, by all accounts, a good guy. He was my neighbor and my tenant, and I didn't even know if he was gay. Regardless, Uncle Jeff was right. Time to let people help me. Time to move out the trash and move into my new life.

Manuel

"¡ANTONIO, DESPIÉRTATE!"

"¿Um, Tío, qué?"

"¿Por que?" I emphasized the word. "Like I told you last night, we're going to go help the landlord clean out his house."

"*Pero* it's Saturday. I need more sleep."

"You have three minutes before I send your mamá in with a pitcher of cold water, and trust me, you don't want to have to hang your sheets up to dry this early in the morning."

Antonio opened one eye and said, "You wouldn't dare."

"She's downstairs filling the pitcher."

"You're evil, Tío, *malísimo*."

"Sí, but you love me."

Antonio didn't chuckle like usual, but then he was fifteen and it was four thirty in the morning.

I slipped downstairs and found my sister-in-law standing at the stove cooking breakfast. "You didn't have to get up at four to make us breakfast."

"No es molestia, hermano. I was awake, and I like to see my poor son dragged out of bed this early. Reminds me of my childhood."

I laughed. María was a first-generation Mexican American, just like us. Whereas my brothers and I had been born to an American mother, María came to America on an asylum visa. She and her family had worked her entire childhood in the fields of Southern California before she met my brother Carlos and the two fell madly in love.

"*¿Qué conoces de ese hombre?*" María asked in Spanish.

"Only that he owns the land we need for cattle grazing until we have rain."

"So, this is to appease el gabacho?"

I laughed. María had a way of never beating around the bush. "I'm helping a neighbor who happens to be in a bad situation."

She stopped and turned toward me. "¿Entonces, es guapo?"

"You are relentless, María," I said and stood up to kiss my sister-in-law on the cheek.

"Hey," Carlos said as he entered the kitchen. "Don't be kissing on my woman, *carnal*."

"Someone has to," I said and playfully poked him in his stomach with my elbow as I walked by.

"And you think she'd be wanting that kiss to be coming from you when she has such a handsome husband as me?"

"Of course," I said, "I am the best-looking brother, after all." I laughed when my go-to jab for my brother didn't get the desired effect. Instead María giggled when Carlos swept her into his arms and kissed her squarely on the mouth.

I loved how much my brothers adored their wives. Even Martín and Cassie were peas in a pod, although poor Cassie didn't understand a word of Spanish and often looked confused when the three of us would go at each other. Luckily, Martín would always sidle up and tell her what we'd said.

As I headed up to see if my nephew had gotten out of bed, I saw him slump out of his room and into the bathroom. I turned into my room and, because I was foolish, I combed my hair again and splashed myself with the subtle cologne I usually only used after a shower.

I had no doubt even in the morning, when it wasn't as hot, I'd be smelly once I was covered in sweat. I didn't want the young landlord to think of me as smelly. I had no idea if he was gay, but that didn't matter. It was about my pride, not attracting the man. Regardless, I'd be damned if I showed up at his house smelling like a cattle farmer, even if that's exactly what I was.

When Antonio and I climbed into the truck, my nephew sniffed and smiled. "You smell nice, Tío."

"And you smell like a teenager," I said, rolling my window down.

"Don't be mean," he said, but the smile remained. "Oh, how are the cows? You thought they'd be going into labor."

"Nothing yet, but we'll need to keep a close eye on them. It'll be any day now," I said as I drove across the fields, the same route we took every day to get to the barn. It hadn't even crossed my mind to use the actual road, even though it would've been significantly smoother.

We parked at the barn and checked on the pregnant heifers first. Seeing they were okay, we walked toward the house, where the landlord had clearly already started work.

I shook my head at the fact that my heart was beating faster than a kid's on their prom night.

Justin

A LONG, HOT shower at my uncles' house helped ease my sore muscles and the irritation I'd felt all day. We ate pizza, and that cheered me up almost as much as my uncles' bickering and loving banter that seemed to be never-ending. Then I crashed. I was tired, and I knew four thirty the next morning would come way too soon.

I'd already arranged for my uncles to come to the farm whenever they got up. Uncle Jeff was a late sleeper. I'd seen him when he had to get up before dawn, and it wasn't pleasant, so I didn't expect to see them until midmorning or even early afternoon.

I'd already been at it a few minutes when I heard a knock on the front door and opened it to a smiling Manuel and a yawning teenager. "*Hola, señor*, this is my nephew, Antonio. I'm sorry, I haven't yet gotten your name."

I blushed. I had no manners. "I'm Justin Latham. Nice to meet you, Antonio, Mr. López," I said as I shook the nephew's hand and then his handsome uncle's outstretched one.

We all turned at the sound of a truck rumbling and watched as it backed up the long driveway to deliver a dumpster right next to the house. "Wow, that's big."

"Sorry. I didn't know how big you needed, so I asked Pete to bring one of his biggest."

I nodded. "Yeah, that should do it," I said and went to meet the driver.

"Hi, I'm Justin," I said, shaking the man's hand. "Thanks for delivering this on such short notice."

"Hidy yourself, I'm Pete." He shook Manuel's hand. "And no problem. Any friend of Manuel is a friend of mine. Just call down to the dump when you're ready for us to come pick this puppy back up."

"Don't I need to sign something?" I asked, and Pete chuckled as he climbed back into his truck.

"Nah, ain't like you're gonna get anyone else to come pick that up. Like I said, just call when you're ready."

As Pete drove off, I stared after him. I knew I was back in the sticks, but Donny had lived in the sticks too, and if someone delivered a dumpster the size of Delaware in the wee hours of the morning, you signed for it.

"Well," Manuel said, "want us to dump the oil drums first?"

I turned to him. "Um, yeah, if you don't mind. I should probably keep the drums now that we have the dumpster."

Without saying anything, Antonio and Manuel began moving the heavy drums full of what I'd emptied out of the house yesterday. When I offered to help, Manuel said, "No need. We got this. You just decide what you want to keep."

I nodded and walked back into the house, turning on a few more lights as I went. I was glad Uncle Henry decided to keep the electricity on. "What do I want to keep?" I asked myself as I surveyed the space. I'd spent years sitting at the small drop-leaf kitchen table that was now so stained and covered with grime that no amount of scrubbing would ever rescue it. My grandmother's prize curio cabinet had all the glass knocked out. That had happened before I'd even left when my dad came home drunk and mad about something.

Everything in this house had a memory attached to it. Good, from when my grandparents were still alive, and horrible, from when dad went off after their deaths.

A short time later, after I'd decided nothing was worth saving, Manuel and Antonio came in, and I shrugged. "Nothing salvageable. It all has to go."

We cleaned out the first floor, tossing furniture, beer cans, and the general trash my father had let accumulate into the dumpster. Around ten, I heard a vehicle and looked out to see my uncles' car, followed by a nice-looking SUV.

Uncle Henry and Uncle Jeff got out and waited for the SUV's occupants, and I recognized Xander and Rhys from when I lived here before.

Manuel and Antonio also stepped onto the porch as my uncles came up the sidewalk. "Nice to see you, Manuel, and thanks for helping our boy this morning," Uncle Henry said.

"The pleasure's mine," Manuel said and introduced Antonio.

"Have you all met Xander and Rhys?" Uncle Henry asked.

"Yes, at the hardware store," Manuel said as he shook their hands.

"Xander, Rhys, it's nice to see you," I said, confused about why they were here. Both Xander and Rhys were a little older than me.

"The guys have come to help you clean this old place out," Uncle Henry said.

I noticed Xander took Rhys's hand and realized the two were a couple. "I really appreciate this. I-I didn't expect help," I said.

Uncle Jeff breezed past me, saying, "No need to stand out here wasting cool weather. If we're here to work, let's get to it."

I looked at him and then back at Uncle Henry, who shrugged. "Guess he's right," I said. "Thank you all for coming. Nothing's staying, so grab anything and take it to the dumpster."

That day, people came and went. Brandon and Levi, both friends of Xander's. I remembered them being thick as thieves back when I lived here. Both men made excuses for their spouses, saying they were busy with their respective farms. Of course, I caught that Brandon was outing himself to me, which I appreciated. I didn't remember Wilcox as anti-gay or anything, but I didn't remember that many gay people either.

A little after noon, Manuel said they had to check on their pregnant heifers and that he needed to drop Antonio off with his parents. I didn't expect to see him again.

I walked with him to the edge of the yard. "Mr. López, I don't know how to thank you."

"Please, call me Manuel. Come by the house some night this week and let us fix you dinner. You can meet my entire family. Although I warn you, that might be more of a chore than me cleaning out your house."

"Yeah, I'd like that. What night?" I asked.

"Let me ask María and Cassie. They pretty much rule our house, so I wouldn't dare set a time without their permission."

I couldn't help but smile. "Sorta old-fashioned that the women rule the home, huh?"

"Yep, and I like my hair on my head, so I won't go against them either. I'll let you know when I come back."

I groaned internally and said, "I'll be here." I knew that, even if I took all the crap out today, I'd still be here tomorrow, the next day, and many days to come as I figured out how to repair the damage my father had done.

By midafternoon, the house was empty, and the dumpster, larger than half the first floor, was bursting with garbage.

Xander, Rhys, Brandon, and Levi lasted until the heat drove them out, but spending time with them allowed me to get to know them better than when I grew up here. It was nice to have other gay men in town and possible friends close to my own age.

Xander had a contract to fix the county's old covered bridges. Nearby Crawford Bridge had been a refuge during my teen years. It no longer connected a roadway, and I figured it was beyond repair. But according to Xander, the bridge wasn't just salvageable, but the county had bought the land around it to make a little park. "When it's done, it'll be quite a nice place," Xander had said with pride.

I resolved to take a look when I had time, but all I could think of was the half-rotten, sagging local landmark my grandfather used to warn me not to set foot on. Of course, that meant I spent more time than I should've exploring it.

I was glad to hear Xander and the county would be saving the old bridge. I could only hope to do the same for my old farmstead. Rhys found termite damage on one corner of the house, and there had definitely been a few leaks over the years—the downstairs ceiling due to a plumbing issue and the upstairs ceiling due to a leaky roof. It might be more trouble than it was worth to fix, but I felt like I owed it to my grandparents to at least try.

I sat across from my uncles and was pleasantly surprised when Manuel came from the barn to join us on the porch. I smiled when I saw him and couldn't help the thrill that sparked in my chest. I ignored it because I didn't want to let the depression and guilt seep back in.

"So, what now?" Uncle Henry asked.

I shrugged. "Now, since I suspect you purposely invited a contractor to help out," I said, and my uncles looked guilty, "I'm going to ask Rhys to come back out and help me decide how to put the home back to rights."

"So you've decided to invest in the property again?"

"Yeah. Today, as all these gay couples showed up to help, I realized maybe this area isn't as horrible as I remember."

My uncles chuckled and smiled. "Well, it's changed and continues to change. Maybe you should spend time in downtown Wilcox and experience those changes yourself. You won't recognize the place."

"I'd like that. Maybe after I figure out what I'm doing around here," I said.

With that, my uncles stood to go. "Manuel, you're welcome at our house. We're stopping by the Chicken Hut on the way home and picking up a bucket. Join us?"

Manuel's face bloomed with genuine appreciation, making him just that much more attractive. "Thank you, but one of the heifers is in labor, so I have to stay close to the barn," he said.

"As in my barn?" I asked, shocked.

"Yeah, it's cooler down here than at the barn next to our place, so we've kept them here until they calve."

"Cool, can I see?" I asked.

"Sure, I guess," Manuel said.

"Uncle Jeff, Uncle Henry, save me some chicken, but I haven't been around cows in… well, a while."

"I thought you were living on a farm in Iowa," Uncle Jeff said and got an elbow in the stomach from Uncle Henry.

I chuckled at the look Uncle Jeff gave him. "I did, but no cows, and the only neighbor who had them lived several miles away. I've missed being around them."

"Come home whenever you wish," Uncle Henry said as he pulled Uncle Jeff toward the car.

I followed Manuel up to the barn and was surprised to find it in great shape. Someone had done repairs and removed all the debris that had occupied the old building since my grandpa died. "Wow, did you clean all this up?" I asked.

"My brothers and I did, *sí*. Is that okay?"

"More than. It hasn't looked this good… well, I don't remember it ever looking so good."

Manuel smiled. "We were taught to keep our farm clean and free of clutter. My grandfather was a stickler, and so was my father."

Just then, we heard a distressed cow over in the corner. Manuel rushed to where the sound came from and smiled. "Well, it's happening. She's already broken her water." He pointed toward a wet spot on the ground. Turning toward me, he said, "This may take some time, Mr. Latham. Wanna keep me company?"

"Sure, why not?" I said, although every muscle in my body ached from two days of cleaning. "And feel free to call me Justin."

We leaned over the wooden stall and watched the mother move anxiously around the small enclosure.

When she lay down, Manuel slipped into the stall and knelt beside her. "Shh, Mamá," he said, then began speaking to her in Spanish. I took two years of Spanish in high school and a year in college, and I still had no idea what Manuel was saying. So much for higher education.

The poor cow seemed distressed, and I wondered if she was having trouble. I'd helped pull more than a few cows out of their moms when my grandpa was around. Of course, back then, I was still pretty small, and he'd tease me that I should be careful not to get sucked in. The memory struck me with both fondness and sadness.

Those were the good years.

Just then I saw two feet and the front of a snout stick out of the cow and hang there for a few seconds before disappearing again. "Whoa, is it okay? Do you need to pull it out?" I asked, causing Manuel to chuckle.

"No, it's pretty normal, and the calf is presented well. It'll come and go a few more times, probably, but it shouldn't take too long now."

True to his word, the calf popped out and in several times before the mom finally pushed it out onto the ground.

She immediately got up and began licking her calf. "Aah, that's a good mamá." Manuel patted her side as he left the stall and motioned for me to follow.

He quickly checked on the other two cows, and since neither seemed to be aware there was anything amiss, he led me out of the barn. "They'll be okay tonight. I'll go back in to make sure the calf is suckling, but for now, it's best to leave them alone so they can bond."

I nodded. "It's been a long time since I saw that in real life," I said as I leaned against the side of the barn. "My grandpa raised cows, and I used to help him. Unfortunately, when he died, my father sold them, and since then, he let the property run down. I haven't been very hands-on since."

"You seemed not to mind it," Manuel said.

"I don't, not really. I was never what you'd call a rancher or cowboy. I tended to do better helping keep the house together than I was out herding cattle," I said, laughing.

Of course, that was an understatement. Even though I enjoyed being around the cows, I hated the never-ending hard work associated with repairing fences, finding and bringing back cows that got out of the pen, and especially avoiding angry bulls.

"Come on. That took less time than I thought, and your uncles wanted you to see Wilcox. We can grab a soda at the service station and celebrate a good day for both of us."

I thought about saying yes, but it felt too much like a date. "I appreciate the offer, Manuel, but I should probably get back."

"Oh, then I'll see you on Tuesday?"

"Tuesday?" I asked.

Manuel sighed. "I forgot to tell you. María, my *cuñada*, wishes you to come to dinner on Tuesday. Do you like *gallina pinta*?" he asked.

I shrugged. "No idea, what is it?"

"Soup, made out of oxtail. Has beans and hominy too."

I smiled. "Dang, I haven't had hominy since my grandmother was alive."

"So, do you like it?"

"Sure, I think so. I don't remember not liking it."

"Good, then I'll see you Tuesday?"

"Sí," I said, at least remembering how to say yes in Spanish, and headed back toward the house.

Manuel and his family were people I wanted to know. I could already tell he was a good man, and if he and Antonio were any indication of how the rest of the family were, I would enjoy getting to know all of them.

Manuel

THE OTHER cows gave birth the following day, and even though none had trouble, having to be at the barn to watch them put me off my schedule. The times I checked the house, Justin was nowhere to be seen.

Oh well, on Tuesday, we had a date. Okay, not exactly a date, but he would be joining me for dinner. I didn't know if he was gay, but if he was, he either had no interest in me or wasn't ready yet. He hadn't given me the cold shoulder the night the first calf was born, but the air still felt chilly.

Regardless, I liked him, and he was our landlord and neighbor. It would do us good to get to know him and build a friendly relationship.

"WE NEED to sell some cows. Sales at the butcher shop are down, and the price of hay is skyrocketing," Martín said as the family sat down for dinner. Of course, that had been Martín's stance since the beginning of March.

"I'm afraid I'm almost in agreement," Carlos said. "I don't know how we can possibly keep up with feeding hay in the summer as well as the decrease in business."

"If we sell now, we stand to lose close to a hundred grand," I reminded them. "Beef prices are down all over the country. I still say we need to hold out and hope for rain or a break in the weather. Besides, the holidays will hopefully bump up sales at the store. Then we need to get to Labor Day, and the worst of the heat should subside."

María, who seldom chimed in, said, "I'm inclined to agree with Manuel. I don't want to take the loss on selling, but we should also try to think outside the box. Mrs. Simpson, with the *Northport Tribune*, gave me an idea. Wilcox does a big celebration every Memorial Day weekend, and last year, the vendor who usually brings *la carne asada* y *las costillas* dropped out."

"I'm not sure how that helps," Carlos said, and she held her hand up.

"That's because you've not let me finish, husband."

Carlos nodded, and María continued. "They sold over two hundred briskets the last time they were here. The paper even did a big article, saying how many people went just for the carne asada."

"So, what? You think we could supply the brisket for whoever takes over?" Martín asked, and got a nasty look from our sister-in-law.

"No, *menso*, we will supply *and* cook the meat."

"Wait, we haven't done a carne asada before, at least not on that scale," Carlos said.

"And isn't this the perfect time to start?" she asked. "When we have an overstock of frozen meat we can't sell and there's clearly a hunger for a *carne asada al carbón* in these parts?"

"They already have a barbecue restaurant in Northport, and one just outside Junction Basin," Antonio said.

"Yes," Cassie said, and she smiled and seemed surprised when we all turned to her. "I've been learning Spanish. I can understand," she said. "They only serve pulled pork at both restaurants. No one around here serves Western-style barbecue. You have to go to the bigger cities for that."

Martín beamed at his wife and would've gotten up to kiss her had Carlos not held him down. "Cassie, you have a point," he said. "Why don't we do an experiment? We'll let the folks in town know we're going to smoke some meat and sell it in the shop, and if it sells okay, we'll bid for the Wilcox sale over the holiday."

We all agreed, and after supper I went to my room and reviewed the numbers on my spreadsheet. We had so many steers that should've been sold by now and many more that we planned to slaughter for the butcher shop throughout the year.

I hadn't mentioned it to the guys downstairs, because if we sold instead of slaughtered ourselves, the losses would be so great it would probably put us out of business. I'd been trying to figure out how to get us out of the hole.

María's suggestion was good. I'd considered it myself, but I was afraid that selling smoked meats at the shop, even if we sold over two hundred briskets, wouldn't be enough to get us out of the slump.

I'd been talking to our father in El Paso because I knew he wouldn't tell my brothers until I'd had time to figure it out, and he knew the cattle industry inside and out. In the nineteen eighties, our papá and grandparents had helped open the export of beef from Mexico into the US.

Papá was talking to his old contacts, hoping to find someone to help us unload several hundred head of cattle without such intense losses. So far, both he and I had come up empty-handed.

Determined to take my mind off the crisis, I closed my laptop and let myself think of the handsome landlord, just over the pastures from where I currently lay. Well, maybe not. The house was still a shack, but he'd be there soon enough.

I'd dated an older guy three years ago, and he and I had something on and off for a year after we broke up, but since then, I hadn't had time or access to men I was interested in. I took a deep breath and let it out slowly. It would be nice to date someone so close. I shook my head. Oh well, time would tell, and Tuesday night he was coming to dinner. Maybe when we weren't covered in dirt or lurking in a barn while a cow gave birth, I would get a better picture of whether or not Justin was interested.

Justin

WHEN RHYS told me the cost of rehabbing the old home, I almost swallowed my tongue. I asked him to repeat it to ensure I hadn't misunderstood, and I shook my head at the thought of spending that much money on the old farmstead.

With his architect stepfather's help, we planned to move a wall, completely replace the kitchen and bathroom, and repair the sunroom on the back that my grandparents had added. Given I was in Bumfuck, Oregon, however, I wasn't sure I'd ever recoup the investment when I sold the place.

I asked my uncles their opinions when I shared the plans and estimates with them that night, and they laughed. "Son, do you not know how much that farm's worth?"

"Two hundred to two hundred fifty thousand?" I asked.

Both men continued chuckling. "Try five to six hundred thousand," Uncle Henry said.

My eyes bugged out of my head. "No way. For that old piece of land?"

"Probably more now with all the development happening in and around Wilcox."

"I know for a fact if you listed it, you'd be able to sell for five fifty, and that's before we even advertised it. I had more than one person ask while it was still in probate."

"Really?" I asked. "So, one fifty for renovations isn't too much?"

Uncle Henry sighed. "Son, Rhys is doing you a favor, doing it that cheap. He could probably charge at least a third more. He and Xander are in high demand these days."

"Why is he doing me a favor? I mean, I remember him and Xander, but it's not like we were friends back then."

"'Cause you're our family, and they've become close to us since they moved back to town. I'm guessing they also know how much you've had to overcome, considering who your dad was."

I slumped in my chair. "I don't want charity."

"They aren't offering charity. I didn't mean it like that." Uncle Henry came to sit beside me. "Justin, folks around here have always taken care of their own. Of course, who they consider their own might be in question from time to time, but I assure you, if those guys didn't like you, not only would they be charging you a pretty penny, but I doubt you could've convinced them to even agree to the project. Last I heard, they had three other contracts in the pipeline from millionaires moving this way from the Portland area. People in Wilcox love to gossip about such things, after all."

"So, you think I should accept?" I asked, feeling apprehensive and concerned that the money I received from Donny's life insurance was being spent too quickly.

"I think it would be a wise investment. Even if you decide to sell, renovating the home would make it much more valuable. And if you decide to stay, you deserve to have a nice place. I can't help but think my sister would be over the moon, thinking that old home would finally be getting the glam-up it deserves."

"Mom liked it there, didn't she?" I asked.

Uncle Henry beamed. "She did indeed. Loved your grandmother and grandpa too, although she told them they were old coots more than a few times to their faces."

"It's too bad she sucked at choosing men," I said with a sigh.

"Oh well, you didn't know your dad back then. He was handsome and smart and loved your mom so much." He frowned. "Both Jeff and I think losing your mom and then his parents broke him inside."

"And I wasn't enough—"

"That's enough of that," Uncle Henry cut in. "Your dad is responsible for his own wickedness. That's not on you, you hear me?" Then he turned in his chair to face me and waited until I made eye contact. "Even when you lose someone—someone as special as my sister—you stand up and dust yourself off, especially when you have a little one depending on you. Losing someone you love doesn't give you the right to take that pain out on somebody else."

Uncle Jeff put his hand on Uncle Henry, whose eyes were still alight with a fiery anger that I knew had been building since my father started laying hands on me. "I'm in the same place he once was," I said around a lump in my throat. "Now I'm the one who lost someone, and I'm wallowing in self-pity."

"Shit," Uncle Henry said. "Son, I didn't mean you shouldn't mourn. Grieving is normal and necessary. Otherwise it'll eat you up inside like it did your dad."

I let out a watery laugh. "No, you're right. Donny was the last person who'd want me to become like my father just 'cause I lost him." I took a deep breath and let it out slowly. "It's just I miss him. We barely had time to start a life together." I shook my head. I'd said the same thing multiple times since I came home. But that was the crux of it. It felt like we'd only just found each other and then I'd lost him for good.

"Did Dad feel that way after Mom died? He'd just gotten her, only to lose her?" I asked.

Uncle Henry looked sad. "I don't know, son, he never said. Truth is, he didn't talk much after she died. Your grandparents did, of course, and they always welcomed me into their home. But I know some of the light went out of him after Shelia died."

"It's hard not to blame myself for her loss, same as it's hard not to blame myself for his going off on me. I know"—I put my hand up to stop the argument—"but it's hard to convince that little boy he wasn't somehow responsible for all this."

Uncle Jeff had been listening to our conversation and moved his hand from covering Uncle Henry's to mine. "I used to blame myself for the abuse I suffered too, and it took years of therapy for me to get to the point where my brain and heart lined up about it. But you hold on to this truth. Adults are responsible for children, not the other way around."

I knew Uncle Jeff had been abused when he was little and then had gone to live with his aunt and uncle, only to be kicked out when he turned seventeen. The church he attended in Iowa had sent him to college in Lamoni, which he said had saved him.

He rarely spoke about it, and the fact that he was speaking about it now made me feel honored and loved. It was a feeling I always had when I was around my uncles, but knowing Uncle Jeff trusted me with that part, even in a small way, magnified that.

"Thanks, Uncle Jeff," I said. Then I stood and hugged them both. "I think I'm gonna turn in early. Lots of emotional ups and downs these past few days—not just about Donny, but cleaning out the house and talking about turning it into something new. It's amazing and sad too. I guess that's just how change works, huh?"

Both men nodded, and I quickly dashed upstairs to avoid tearing up yet again. I had lost a lot over the years, and by all counts, I should be fucked up a hell of a lot more than I was. I was blessed much more than I was cursed.

"GRACIAS," I SAID as María served me a bowl of soup. It smelled amazing. Cassie brought in a platter with soft tacos filled with what looked like carne asada. My mouth watered.

We joined hands as soon as everyone was seated, and Carlos asked for the blessing in Spanish. I wondered why I didn't feel awkward. I almost always felt out of place, especially when I would eat with Donny's family. I had to guess it was because of how accommodating this family was.

Everyone dove in then, and I smiled. This was how it'd been at mealtimes when I was growing up with my grandparents—prayer first, then a free-for-all.

"Antonio, you don't touch that until Señor Latham has his."

The teenager looked appropriately chastised, and I winked at him as I took one of the tacos and placed it next to the bowl on my plate. "I recommend you take another," Manuel said. "Once his mother unleashes him, he'll eat everything on the table."

Antonio eyed his uncle but didn't argue. I did as Manuel recommended and then looked at María, who nodded.

The boy proved to be a bottomless pit. At fifteen, he was already taller than me and stouter. I guess that came from working on the farm with his family.

"So, Justin, what do you do for a living?" Cassie asked.

"Well, not much for a while. I lived with my boyfriend on a farm in Iowa until recently. I was more of a house husband than anything else."

"But," Antonio said, looking confused, "didn't you say you went to college in Iowa?"

I laughed. "Yes, I have a bachelor's degree in history, which is mostly worthless when it comes to making a living. I'm afraid I'm not much good for anything other than taking tests and smoking meats."

The entire table went silent and looked at me. I froze and wondered what I'd said wrong.

"You know how to smoke meat?" Manuel asked.

I nodded. "Yes, before I met my late boyfriend," I began, then hesitated. Could you call your deceased boyfriend your late boyfriend, like a late husband? I shook off the thought. "I learned how to smoke meat from my father. I also worked for a catering company for several months in Iowa and they catered only smoked meats... you know, barbecue."

"Late boyfriend?" María asked. I was hoping they'd missed that detail.

"Yes." I took a fortifying breath. "He was killed while working on the farm. His combine fell into a large canyon."

Another hush fell over the table. I glanced at the sympathetic faces staring back at me and wished I could take back the whole depressing conversation. I'd just decided to put that behind me, move past it so I didn't end up like my drunk-ass father, and the first thing I did when I met new friends was bring it up.

"Well, señor, we've all loved and lost," Martín said. "But we've not lost them in that way. We are all very sorry for that. Que en paz descanse."

I smiled. "Thank you." I resumed eating and prayed someone would change the subject to break the awkwardness I'd created.

"So, tell us about your ability to smoke meat," Carlos said, and María slapped him on the arm while Cassie shook her head. "What? We all want to know."

That piqued my curiosity. "Why?"

Manuel sighed. "You'll have to forgive us, Justin. We're in a crisis with the cattle. The drought has slowed sales at our butcher shop, and the price of beef is down by almost half since last spring. We are considering selling smoked meats to increase revenue."

"So you need to hire a smoking expert and that person is me?" I asked and winked at Manuel.

He chuckled. "Are you looking for a job?"

"That would be a hell yes. Oh!" I said and covered my mouth. "I didn't mean to swear. You'll have to forgive me. I haven't been in polite company in a while."

Carlos and Martín laughed. "Neither have any of us, but thanks for thinking of us that way," Manuel said. "Seriously, you know how to smoke meats on a large scale?"

I nodded. "Yeah, that's the one thing my dad did pretty often when he wasn't drunk. We'd smoke a whole hog, brisket, ribs, you name it."

"You're hired," Antonio said right before stuffing his face with the last of the carne asada tacos.

The entire table chuckled, except for María, who was just coming back from the kitchen.

"Why don't you all come by the house this weekend before the rehab crew tears into it? I'll smoke up some meats, and you can see if I'm up to the task."

"Really?" Manuel asked.

"Sure, why not? I'm sure my father's gigantic smoker is somewhere on the property. I just haven't laid eyes on it yet. It's one of the few things the man valued enough to take care of properly."

"So long as you cook it, we'll supply the meat," María said.

"And the beverages," Manuel offered with a grin.

"Bring your backs too, 'cause there's always a ton of wood to cut." I returned his grin before I let curiosity get the better of me. "Just so we're clear, you all haven't smoked meat before? Despite owning a cattle business and running a butcher shop?"

Carlos sighed. "Well, yes and no. We didn't grow up with much money, and cows were sold, not butchered. Most of our meals in El Paso were chicken."

"Or no meat at all," Martín chimed in.

"Right, or no meat at all," Carlos agreed. "We know how to raise them. We know how to slaughter them, although we have to use a professional USDA-approved place now. We even know how to butcher and cook them, but smoking, not so much. And certainly not on a large scale."

I smiled and let myself feel excited about hosting guests at the farm for the first time ever. "I'd be happy to show you how it's done."

"Can you do it on Sunday?" Manuel asked. "That's the only day the butcher shop is closed."

"No reason why not. In fact, why don't we invite more people? Let's make it a party."

Everyone around the table smiled and nodded, and Antonio started rattling off names of friends he wanted to invite.

I leaned toward Manuel, who was sitting beside me, and quietly thanked him for having invited me to dinner with his family. I really liked these folks. More than I even hoped I would.

Manuel

"HOW MANY people are coming?" I asked Justin over the phone. "María wanted me to find out how many briskets to remove from the freezer."

"Twenty-five that I know of," he responded. "Plus however many friends your nephew invited."

"So you need what? Five, six briskets?"

"Three should be fine, but if you've got ribs, bring me a few racks. People always like ribs to go with their brisket." I could tell Justin was calculating in his head by the unsure way he responded.

"Not a problem," I said. I wanted to find an excuse to stay on the phone a few moments longer, but I didn't try. He'd recently lost his lover, so I now understood why a sense of sadness clung to him.

When I hung up, I updated María, then drove over to Justin's barn to release the three heifers and their calves into the pasture. I'd decided to keep them in the barn for several days with the excuse of ensuring the moms were well-fed while they had the little ones, but in truth, I wanted every excuse to run into Justin.

I was being a fool. The man had a life. Even if he was cleaning out the dilapidated house, he lived with his uncles in town. Why should I expect he'd be here at any given time?

As I watched the cows rejoin the herd, I heard crashing metal and cussing from the old shed.

I rushed there and found Justin sucking his thumb. "You okay?" I asked.

"Yeah, just cut my thumb on a piece of old tin. Damn, I was supposed to get a tetanus booster, but with Don—"

A cloud crossed Justin's face, and I suspected his mind had turned to his deceased lover. "What can I do to help?" I quickly asked, hoping to keep his mind in the present.

"I'm trying to get to my dad's smoker. I think it's buried back here under all this tin roofing."

"How can you be sure?" I asked as I looked at the pile in front of me.

He bent down, gestured for me to do the same, and pointed. "That, I believe, is the wheel to the smoker."

"Oh, let me help you, then," I said, and we began to pull the sheets of tin off the smoker. Of course, too many years of my own father lecturing me about being organized on the farm forced me to stack it neatly to the side.

When Justin noticed, he laughed. "You're a bit OCD, huh?"

"Oh no. My father was a stickler for keeping things organized. It's been ground into my head since I could walk. I think the fact that I'm ADHD made it that much more important to do things right the first time so I didn't screw it up and cause my family to have to go back and fix my mistakes."

"Sounds harsh," Justin said, and I shook my head.

"No, never harsh, just high expectations. I have wonderful parents. Wish I could talk them into moving here."

"Really?" he asked. "Where are they?"

"El Paso. Papá is very attached to the little house he purchased there, and Mamá still works at a local hotel. Her best friend married Mr. Lancaster, and he hired my brothers and me to work on the farm we now own. That's how we ended up here in Wilcox."

"How did you afford to buy it?" he asked, then blushed. "I'm sorry, I didn't mean to pry. It's just I didn't realize my property was worth what it is until a few days ago. I suspect your farm is just as valuable."

"No need to apologize. We pooled our resources. Carlos owned a home in El Paso, and between selling it, and Martín's and my savings, we had the money to buy the place outright by the time Mr. Lancaster and his wife were ready to retire to Florida."

"Impressive," he said. "Now you're trying to become big cattle farmers."

I chuckled. "Trying and failing, since it seems like everything is against us. The fluctuating price of cattle, heat waves, meandering bulls—"

He cocked an eyebrow, and I laughed. "Those three little calves?" I pointed toward the herd. When he nodded, I continued, "Those should be registered calves born next spring, but Mr. Morris's bull snuck in last fall, and well, there's the result."

Justin's eyes twinkled as he said, "Boys will be boys."

"I guess," I responded and pulled the final sheet of tin off the enormous smoker. "Anyway, why did your dad bury this under all that roofing?"

"Probably to keep it from being stolen while he was passed out drunk."

"Ouch, you don't have a good opinion of your father, do you?"

"He didn't give me many reasons to, no. But I'm coming to terms with it. Meanwhile, what do you think?" he asked as he gestured to the impressive equipment.

"Wow, it looks new."

"That's 'cause he babied this thing like it was his child. Well, better, truth be told."

Justin lifted the lid and surveyed the smoker. "Still in great shape. He kept the thing well-oiled on the outside, and even though it stayed out in all weather, it's cast iron, so the oil kept it waterproof. He'd occasionally take the pressure washer to the inside, but that was only to keep it from becoming a fire risk. Once I thought I'd help him, so I used Dawn dish soap in the pressure washer, and my dad about came undone."

He chuckled and turned to me. Realizing I didn't get it, he added, "Smokers season over time. The oils that collect there harden and become part of the cooking process. Come here. Smell the inside."

I leaned in close and caught a whiff of smoked meat. "That's what the meat will taste like, and if you use Dawn, it takes all that off and can even cause the smoker to rust. There's your first lesson on smoking meats. Smoke them on a well-seasoned smoker."

I could've stayed with Justin all day, picking up tips and simply enjoying his company, but I needed to pick Antonio up from the shop and spread some hay around the upper pasture for the cows.

"Hey, help me move this over to the house so I can start it up. I don't dare use it over here since there's so many trees around. With this heat wave, I'm likely to burn the countryside down," he said.

"No, don't do that. I've got too much to lose," I said in a tone more serious than I'd intended.

He nodded. "You do indeed."

Once the smoker was behind the old house, Justin clipped a hose onto a pressure washer and began spraying down the inside. When he was done, he left it open to air out.

"So this does a good job smoking meat?" I asked as I eyed the strange-looking contraption.

"Son," Justin said in a deeper voice than his own, "this here's what you call a Lang smoker. There's a time when these weren't as well-known as they are now. My dad and I, we went all the way to Georgia to pick this little beauty up." He smirked and patted the thing like it was made of gold.

I enjoyed seeing the man's playful side. "Your dad really loved it, didn't he."

"Oh yeah, and I'm gonna guess, once you eat the meat I cook on Sunday, you're gonna love it too."

I hung out for as long as I could as Justin filled the smoker with wood and lit it. He closed it then and waited for the smoker to heat up.

"That's it?" I asked.

Justin's face cracked with his smile. "No, it's only the beginning. I don't know how long it sat out here unused, but I'm guessing a while. I want to get a good fire started to sterilize it. Then on Sunday, all we've got to do is load it and start cooking."

"Okay, you're the boss."

"Well, if you like my meat," Justin said, "you could be the boss."

I could see the moment he realized he'd said that out loud, because he blushed adorably. Since any doubts I might've harbored about his sexuality had been washed away at the dinner at my house, I wasn't about to let the flirty comment slide.

"I don't think there's gonna be any question how I feel about your meat, but you know, one shouldn't rush things." His blush deepened, and I pointed to the smoker. "That's also true when it comes to cooking."

I left shortly after.

I liked Justin, a lot, and I wasn't joking, but I could give him all the time he needed.

Justin

My Freudian slip left me mortified. Geez, I sounded like a bad porn movie. I'd nearly recovered enough to try to save face when Manuel quickly signed, sealed, and stamped confirmation of his interest. And it seemed he was willing to give me time.

Even after he left, my face glowed, and I couldn't help but think Donny was somewhere laughing his ass off.

I needed to cool off, so I headed to where our little stream merged with the larger river. I'd spent many a boyhood day swimming in the stream by the covered bridge. At this time of year, it was usually too cold, but the recent unseasonable warmth and dryness made a swim possible.

I expected the area to be overgrown, but the cows had done a good job keeping the grass down. Luckily, the stream wasn't visible from the old bridge or the soon-to-be park Xander had mentioned, so I could come here and enjoy myself without concern. I stripped and climbed into the cool water, pleased that the years of runoff hadn't filled in the deep spot where I'd always loved to swim when I was young.

I sighed with relief from the intense heat and let myself float to the surface as I thought about Manuel and Donny and how different they were. Manuel was laid-back and easygoing where Donny was gregarious. Everyone who knew him loved him. At six foot five, he towered over me, and I reveled in tracing with my fingertips every outline of his strong Norwegian features. Donny had been the love of my life, and that love had been hot and instant.

We were going to have a long and loyal life together. Now that he was gone I wondered if I would feel that way again. And I wondered if it could be with someone like Manuel. I knew I'd never date a man who even remotely resembled or reminded me of my Donny.

No matter what happened in my future, Donny would always hold part of my heart, and I had no desire to replace him. And if I ever loved another person, he would have to come to terms with my love for Donny.

I climbed out of the water and laughed when a group of cows moved into the grove to enjoy the shade and cooling effect of the stream.

One of the calves bounded around its mom, looked at me, and then dashed back under its mom's legs.

I chuckled as I pulled my clothes back on. "You might be a mutt, but you're mighty cute," I said to him as I navigated around the herd and back up to the house to check on the smoker. The fire was beginning to die down, so I used the hose to put out the coals and wash out the firebox. Then I picked up my phone, called the health clinic in town, and asked about getting a tetanus shot.

Not everything about this place was horrible. I had my uncles and my friends here, or at least I was developing friendships.

With Dad gone, it felt like the farmstead could be a source of pride... with a little time and effort. To my surprise, the prospect no longer filled me with resentment and dread.

It was the first time I'd felt that way since my grandmother passed over ten years ago.

I could envision building a life for myself here—a contented, purposeful, fulfilling life, regardless of my painful past or if I had a loving partner alongside me.

Manuel

MARÍA INSISTED Justin should smoke five briskets so we had some left over for home. In the end, that saved our asses. I hadn't seen so many people in one place since my cousin's *quinceañera* seven years ago.

Even with the extra brisket and twelve racks of ribs, all the meat was gone before the evening ended.

The same people who'd shown up to help clean out Justin's house were all here, but so were a lot of others I hadn't met before.

Folks came and went throughout the day, and most brought food, so there were mounds of sides. Occasionally Justin would scoop up some sides and take them to María. The third time I saw him do it, I wandered over to hear what he was telling her. "This is a simple dish too. Unlike the beans that need a long time to cook, mac and cheese can be cooked in the oven, stored in plastic containers, and sold out of the refrigerator."

They were talking about a menu? "Are we opening a restaurant?" I asked, and María and Justin looked at me as if I'd interrupted top secret negotiations.

"No," María said, exasperated. "But Justin does have a point. If we serve *carne ahumada*, *tortas*, and other main dishes, we need sides for people to buy, not just potato chips."

Justin nodded at my sister-in-law and shrugged at me. "Country people have expectations, and smoked meat is fancy eating. If you serve brisket, they will expect a few sides to go with it."

"And how much can we charge for all this?" I asked, concerned we were getting in over our heads.

"If we serve food that tastes good, we can easily get fifteen dollars a plate. Maybe more."

"People will pay that?" I asked.

Justin laughed. "Have you seen the price of beef lately?" I had. A small brisket in even the discounted big box stores in Eugene sold for over thirty bucks. Brisket cooked down to nothing too, so it made sense that we'd have to charge that much per plate.

"Well, if you think it'll sell."

"Look around," Justin said. "See all these people? Look over there. That's Ellen Petterson. I remember her from when I was little. See how she closes her eyes when she takes a bite? That means she's really enjoying it. Then over there, see that guy? I don't remember his name, but he's from New York. Some doctor who retired and moved out here to be closer to his grandchildren. He looks like he could run off to Tahiti with that sandwich."

I smiled. "But how do we get them to visit our butcher shop?"

"That I don't know. I'm not a marketing guy, but that lady over there? That woman runs the marketing side of one of our local wineries. I'm almost sure, the way she's tearing into those ribs, if we cook her up some brisket, we can sweet-talk her into helping."

Seeing people devour the products of our labor made the day's efforts worth it. Eventually, I let go of business talk and enjoyed the event with everyone else. Before I knew it, Dalton and Pierce, who ran an agribusiness operation together on the other side of Wilcox, came over and put a beer in my hand.

"So," Dalton said after we'd been chatting for a while, and I could tell he was about to tease me, "I hear you might have a bit of a thing for young Justin Latham over there."

"Oh, word does get around, doesn't it?" I asked, not denying it but looking for a way out of the conversation before I got in too deep.

"Don't worry, we aren't going to spill the beans, but we have a favor to ask."

I looked back and forth between the two men I'd begun to think of as potential friends. "What?" I asked.

"Well, you see…." Dalton said and paused for effect.

"Get on with it before the man dies of old age," Mayor Polly said as she approached us, plate of ribs in hand.

"You can really ruin a guy's momentum," he said, and Polly laughed.

"My nephew is trying to ask if your family is going into catering because they have three weddings coming up, and all three have requested barbecue. Barbecue that we have to order from Eugene, then, on the day of each wedding, pick up, transport here, and keep warm while still hosting."

I'd forgotten they turned their covered bridge into a wedding chapel. Cassie had just attended a wedding there and couldn't stop talking about it or about wanting to turn the ramshackle bridge downstream from us into a similar event venue. Never mind that we didn't own land anywhere near the bridge, let alone the span itself.

I shrugged. "To be honest, catering is Justin and María's thing, but come with me, and we can ask."

María and Justin eyed each other the entire time Dalton explained what he and Pierce were looking for. I listened as they asked questions about how many guests, how much food, and how much time they'd have to pull it off. When the conversation turned to the budget, I almost laughed at the dollar signs that all but popped into their eyes.

"For real, consider it," Dalton chimed in. "It's something we're getting more and more requests for, and the restaurant in Eugene refuses to deliver. If someone local was doing it, it would make our lives a whole lot easier. Not to mention, supporting fellow hometown businesses is important to us."

"Not only that, but your barbecue kicks their asses," Pierce said and got a nasty look from Dalton, likely because Pierce had cussed in front of the mayor, although she was nodding so hard I thought she might put her neck out.

"Let us think about it," María said. "When do you need our answer?"

"Sooner is better, but how about next Friday?"

"That should work," María said. When the trio walked off, I saw Justin and María exchange smiles.

I sighed. "So, this is happening?"

"Oh, this has already happened," Justin said.

After the event wound down, cleanup required minimal effort. Not only did several folks stay behind to help, but Rhys and Xander piled the trash bags into the back of their pickup and hauled them away. By the time my family and Justin collapsed on the front porch, the place looked the same as it did any other day.

"That was intense," Antonio said, and everyone nodded.

"So," María said as she made eye contact with Justin, "when can you start?"

"I think I already have," he said, and a collective agreement seemed to pass through the group.

"I agree. So, tomorrow, then?" she asked.

"We'll need to move the smoker up to your butcher shop and get everything squared with the health department. Want me to come by tomorrow and help get that paperwork rolling?"

"That is an absolute yes," Cassie said. "If he doesn't, then we all know I'll have to, and I hate dealing with them."

Martín laughed, leaned over, and kissed his wife on the neck. "Amor, you are being overworked by these barbarians."

"¿Edá?" She laughed and leaned back against her husband.

They chatted about catering and improving business in the butcher shop, but I didn't dare hope this would be the answer to our overstock of cattle. But if it reduced the amount of stock, it might be enough for us to squeak by until better times returned.

Justin

I HAVE NEVER had as much fun starting a job in all my life. Building a food service into the existing butcher shop was a breeze. We already had the required sinks and refrigeration. Since most of the prepared foods would be displayed in the public shopping area, there were no issues about keeping raw and cooked food together.

We had to purchase more coolers for the front, but Carlos made one phone call, and they were delivered by the afternoon of my first day.

Manuel had his buddy, Pete, the same guy who delivered the dumpster, pick up my smoker and move it to the butcher shop. By the following Monday, I was cooking sides and smoking meat.

By eleven thirty, we were sold out, and more than one very disappointed customer came in, upset that we didn't better prepare for the rush. Apparently word had traveled at lightning speed.

María thought fast and gave everyone who'd missed out a 10 percent discount coupon for the following day. We then tripled the amount of meat served that first day, and promptly ran out at twelve thirty. Again we handed out 10 percent discounts to disgruntled customers.

By Saturday we finally figured out the flow of supply and demand amid the lunch rush, and when María totaled her drawer for the week, she squealed in delight. "Justin, you won't believe this, but we've doubled our weekly sales. Not only our lunch sales but also our other sales."

Laughing, she and Cassie grabbed me and swung me around the room. When Carlos and Martín came in, they accused me of trying to run off with their women. "Oh, that wouldn't be hard, as handsome as I am," I said, and everyone in the room stopped and stared. "What? I've listened to you all go at each other all week. Did you think I couldn't dish it out?"

They all but raised the roof laughing as Carlos, then the others, clapped me on the back and congratulated me on our successful opening week.

"You'll be coming by the house tomorrow for lunch, so don't be trying to get out of it," María said in her no-nonsense way. "The family talks business on Sundays, and since you helped lift us out of this slump, you'll be there to celebrate."

It felt great to be included, and all I could do was smile and nod.

I only worked six-hour days at the butcher shop on Monday through Friday and an eight-hour day on Saturday. Of course, I hung around the shop longer most days because I wanted to spend time with the folks I'd quickly come to think of as friends.

I showed Carlos and Martín how to watch the meat and keep tabs on the temperature so they could keep the process going when I left and ensure everything was smoked to perfection and tender and moist for customers the next day.

I had never had a job where I wanted to hang out with everyone on Sunday, my one day off, but honestly, I would've missed them had I not.

Uncle Henry and Uncle Jeff were in Portland, and after a week of being with the lively bunch, I hated the idea of being alone.

I showed up at the López home at eleven, as instructed, and immediately began helping María prep the food for lunch. When she didn't stop me, I figured I was becoming part of her brood.

We all sat around the dining table, Manuel next to me, just like the first time I came for dinner. After a brief blessing, we dug in.

"María," I said as the flavors burst in my mouth, "if you weren't already married, I'd try to woo you so you could make this for me every Sunday."

Carlos glanced at me with what I'd come to think of as his playful look and said, "*Compadre*, she needs more than you can give."

I opened and shut my mouth, and when the table burst into laughter, I did too. "*Es cierto*, you should stay with Carlos, María," I said, causing more laughs.

Of course, Antonio just sat at the end of the table and shook his head—poor kid.

After lunch I helped clear the table, and before I left to sit with the guys, María pulled me aside. "I may be off the table, but you know our Manuel is not, and he's a good catch, that one."

I heard the pride in her voice, and she sauntered off without looking back. María López was a live wire and pulled no punches. I knew she wanted nothing but the best for her brother-in-law, and apparently she thought I measured up. Unfortunately, I didn't feel ready for that yet.

A relationship with Manuel meant a relationship with these people, and even though he was one of the most handsome men I knew, right now, I needed their friendships more. I wanted to continue building those organically, without the additional layer of romantic entanglement. And I had to make the farmstead feel more like the tranquil home I'd never had. If it all eventually led to a second chance at love, that'd be a bridge for future me to cross.

Manuel

I'D PLANNED to bring up the crisis we were facing at today's meeting, but María had invited Justin, and the family wanted to celebrate coming out of the slump at the butcher shop.

We had three freezers at the shop and two here at the house, all full of meat, so we didn't need to butcher again anytime soon. And I was already running low on hay. Another purchase would wipe out all the profits this week and possibly more.

But as we sat around the dining table, I put aside my concerns and joined the celebratory mood. Once Justin left, I went to my room, crunched the numbers again, and called our papá. "It's getting increasingly difficult to manage all this," I admitted.

"*Mijo*, Carlos told me you were doing well at the butcher shop this week. Do you think that will be enough?"

"It would take a miracle and a lot more sales than we've made this week," I said.

"You have to tell them, mijo," he said, and I nodded, feeling sick.

"Sí, Papá, but they were too happy tonight. I'll tell them next week. Who knows, maybe it will rain, and all our problems will be solved."

"You can't hide from your problems, Manuel. You have to face them," he said, and I knew he was right.

After I hung up, I logged into the website for the co-op we used to order hay and did what I had to do. The cost per bale had gone up another third since the last time I'd bought it. Carlos, who watched our budget like a hawk, would discover my purchase and want answers sooner or later, but at least for now, he could be happy along with the rest of our family.

Justin

THE FOLLOWING morning, we were bombarded with customers. One lady said she drove from Medford because she'd been told the brisket and ham sandwich was the best around. When we sold out at noon this time, María just shrugged and said she was sorry.

We'd gone from desperate to appease our customers to accepting the fact that we would struggle to keep up with the resources at hand.

Every day this week, we added meat to the grill, and finally I told them we were at capacity. "If we want to keep up with demand, we'll have to bring in another smoker," I told Carlos when he came out to join me.

"You don't think this is a fluke that will die down in a week or two?" he asked.

I shrugged. "No idea. All I can do is tell you where we are, not where we might be in a week."

"What would you do?" Carlos asked me. I could tell he was struggling with something.

"Depends. From what we learned last week, we almost made more from food sales than butchered meat sales. If this week is any indication, we'll double that. I'd say, if there's a chance this will continue, we should try to keep up, at least to a point."

Carlos nodded, then turned to go. "Hey, man," I said, stopping him, "what's bothering you?"

He took a deep breath and let it out as he flopped into the plastic chair I put out for when I needed to be outside with the meat.

"We're cash-poor at the moment, and when I looked at smokers comparable to yours, they are at least ten grand."

I grabbed an extra chair and pulled it up next to his. "Listen, as things grow here, I was thinking I'd like to partner with you all. I mean, I have no desire to own my own business. I don't like chasing cash flow or trying to figure out how to do all the minutia that keeps a business running, but I do like working here and seeing the catering side of this place grow."

Carlos chuckled. "Well, you own the smoker, so you're already invested in our business. But I'll call a family meeting tonight and let you know what everyone thinks. If we decide to formally bring you aboard as a partner, have you got the funds to buy another smoker?"

I nodded. "I do, and I'd be happy to invest."

"María isn't gonna like this."

I shook my head. I was almost sure he was right. María would think it was charity or selling her family short. She'd embraced me as an employee, and I already considered her a friend, but I didn't want to be seen as interloping on the family business. Ultimately, it was up to them. There's nothing I could say or do that would help Carlos convince her and the others to take me on, even if the possibility of partnering with this fantastic little family enlivened me more than anything had since I left Iowa.

Manuel

"No, ABSOLUTELY not!" I yelled and pounded my fists on the table.

"Cálmate, carnal," Martín said.

"Don't tell me to calm down," I replied, just to make my point. "It's not fair to ask that man, who we're renting land from, has loaned us his smoker, and has come up with most of the side dishes we are serving, to invest in *our* family's business."

"It won't be just ours. If he takes on the catering side, it'll be part his," Cassie said.

I flopped down into the seat. "You know my opinion."

The entire room erupted in discussion until María lifted her hand. "I would normally agree with you, Manuel, but we're in a tight spot. Carlos told me where our cash reserves are, and unless you want to sell our stock at the depressed price and borrow money, leveraging the farm and all we've worked so hard to build these past few years, working with Justin is not a bad idea."

I stared at my sister-in-law. She was the one who always stood against letting outsiders in. I was sure she would be my ally on this one.

"Why are you so resistant?" Carlos asked with a cocked eyebrow. Everyone's eyes fell on me.

"I told you why."

"No, you gave lame excuses. Try again, only with less bullshit."

I stood up, frustration coursing through me, and stomped off without replying.

I'd never behaved so disrespectfully at a family meeting, and I knew I was acting like a child, but I didn't care. My family knew damned well why I didn't want Justin to join our business. Shit, he was the first guy I'd met that I wanted to pursue, and I hoped with time I could. If he became part of the family's business, I wouldn't… couldn't. It muddied the waters and was too damned big a risk.

"Carnal," I heard from outside my bedroom door.

"*Déjame en paz*, Martín. I need time alone."

Naturally, he ignored me and opened the door. To my surprise, he looked genuinely concerned. "I know you better than that. You hate being alone."

I shook my head. "It apparently doesn't matter what I like, don't like, want, or don't want in this family."

"That's not true either, Manuel. We all hear you and respect your wishes, but are Carlos and María wrong? Are we not facing a major financial crisis right now?"

I couldn't argue with him. Carlos had come to me last night to discuss the money situation, and I'd confessed that we had to make hard decisions and make them fast. Otherwise, we were going to put the entire operation in jeopardy.

"You know we are, Martín, but that doesn't mean we should jump in bed with our neighbor."

Martín chuckled. "What?" he asked when I speared him with a glance. "You know that's the real problem here, and we all get it. We can all see how you feel about him. But that doesn't mean he's still not our best option in all of this."

I flopped back on my bed like I used to do when Martín and I shared a room. Carlos was almost ten years older than me, and I was two years older than Martín. We were all close, but because Martín and I were so close in age, he was my best friend.

"I know it's crazy, and I know it's inevitable, but can't I be pissed about it, just for a minute?" I whined.

"Yeah, of course you can, but the family needs to decide. But you can pout about it as long as you wish."

I flipped him off, and he playfully punched my arm. "I'm gonna go tell them you're on board, okay?"

"Yeah," I said. "But brother, tell them you had to fight me, and you're afraid you're going to have a black eye from when I punched you."

"Sure. I'll rub it real hard too so it looks like you did."

"Thanks, and Martín," I said, propping myself up on my elbows. "Don't tell the others. They might have guessed, but I-I...." I shook my head as I searched for the words. "If we're business partners, I have to give up the idea of it being anything else. So, yeah, let's keep this between us."

Martín turned to go but hesitated. "You know that's not true, right?" he asked.

"What's not true?"

"That you have to give up on you and Justin being more... like... *novios*."

"Yeah, it *is* true. If we try dating and it falls apart and he's a big partner in our family's affairs, what'll happen then? No, como decía nuestra abuela, 'No se caga donde se come.'"

"Ugh, I hated that saying," Martín said. "Always grossed me out. You aren't shitting where you eat, hermano. You like him. Nothing wrong with that. Besides, you're *Señor Responsable*. We all know you'll be stupid and obsessive about it all. But still, don't throw any chances to be with him away just because we all decided to go into business with him."

I shrugged and nodded, although Martín was right. I was sorta *exageradamente responsable* when it came to my family and our business. I wouldn't throw all of it away just for a guy.

Justin

"REALLY? YES, let's do it!" I said as the family group hugged me—everyone except Manuel, who looked like he'd swallowed a cactus. Once everyone else was busy prepping for the day, I caught Manuel before he could leave. "What's wrong?" I asked.

"Nothing, why?" he said, and I could tell from his expression that he wanted to avoid the conversation, which only raised my concern more.

"Listen, do you not want this? Because—"

"No, that's not it." He quickly pulled me out of the shop so his nosy sisters-in-law didn't overhear. "I'm excited, but I—" He sighed. "I like you, Justin. I like you more than just as a neighbor or as our landlord, but if we go into business together, pursuing that won't be an option. Ever. I'm trying to come to terms with that."

I stared, slack-jawed. I knew how he felt but wasn't prepared for him to admit it, not so blatantly. I swallowed hard and nodded. "Manuel, I think you're very handsome, and I'll admit if I'd met you before... well, at a different time...."

Manuel stopped me. "Justin, I know you're still mourning your lover. I didn't want to put pressure on you. I should've kept my mouth shut."

I reached over and put my hand on his. "I get it, and no, you didn't put pressure on me. Nor do I want you ever to feel like you can't tell me something important, especially since we're going to be in business together. But whether this partnership happened or not, I'm not ready to date anyone and may never be. But look at it like this," I said, waiting for him to look at me. "I will be family."

He shook his head as I smiled. "That's true. I guess one should be happy with what one's got."

I rubbed my hand up Manuel's very muscular arm and felt passion blossom in my chest. I quickly pulled my hand away and forced myself not to think about how my body reacted to him. "Okay, I'm going to get back in there, but let's make this work. I want to be friends, and I really like your family."

"Yeah, they like you too. We all do. Okay, I'm going to go back to the farm," he said, and he touched his hat like the old guys around here used to do before they left a room. I wondered if that was a cultural thing he'd picked up here or if they did it in El Paso.

I watched him go and couldn't help but feel regret and guilt. This was a no-win situation. I had just lost the love of my life, and now I'd possibly lost the chance with another wonderful man. I knew I needed time, yet it felt like the universe was conspiring against me.

THE NEXT six weeks flew by. Shortly after I was accepted into the fold, the new smoker arrived and had to be seasoned. Since the brisket was our best seller, I used the new smoker for our ribs and chicken so it wouldn't hurt our main sales if they weren't quite as well-flavored. Luckily, none of our customers seemed to notice.

After the smoker issues were ironed out, with María's approval, I expanded our sides to show her how well we could do with those. Unfortunately, we didn't have the room to expand to include everything I wanted to do, so we chose three sides that tasted the best and made the most profit.

We ran out of sandwiches by early afternoon every day. Even with the new smoker, we were so busy we couldn't keep up. The fact that the butcher shop was also bustling with business made me happy, since it benefited the entire family.

I regularly attended Sunday dinner that doubled as the family business meeting, and at the most recent one, I learned they were going to have to start butchering again. Seeing Manuel's relief made me proud, because I'd helped make it happen.

Manuel admitted he hadn't been sure they would survive, and when he thanked me, he had tears in his eyes. I nodded and had to work not to get emotional myself.

"Eventually—maybe after this summer—we should talk about increasing capacity," I said.

María slapped my hand. "You're as bad as this one," she said, waving toward Manuel. "Know when to celebrate and when to bring up new problems. Today, we celebrate solving the last one."

"Hear, hear!" I said and raised my beer in a toast.

Unfortunately, as the rest of our lives got better, the unspoken tension between Manuel and me grew. Although he was friendly, I could tell he struggled with me being part of his life. I probably needed to pull away and let them have more time together as a family, without me. María would be a pill about that, since she insisted I be there as often as possible, but I needed to respect Manuel's need for more space. With the farmhouse renovation scheduled to be done in a couple of weeks, I'd be moving in soon and figured I could spend more time at home. Whether having an excuse to stay away from Manuel was more for his benefit or my own, I wasn't sure.

Of course, there was the other issue. The more time I spent with Manuel, the more *my* heart seemed to want him. I was having more of a hard time processing my mess of emotions. I loved Donny, missed him daily still, and I knew that if I allowed myself to let Manuel in, that wouldn't change, nor did I think Manuel would expect it to.

Being around him and his family all the time made it difficult, but I had to figure out how to manage those feelings.

Manuel

"THE SHOP is just too small," María said one night at dinner.

"What do you mean too small?" Carlos asked.

"We barely have room for customers to enter the store, and it will get cold soon. What if we lose all our customers because we can't serve them? No, we need more space."

"Where will we get that, María? We're just overcoming a crisis caused by the drought. Can't we make it work?"

She looked Carlos in the eye. "If you want our success to continue, we have to expand."

Justin was visibly absent from the conversation, and I wondered if maybe it had been his idea. He'd mentioned a few weeks ago that we needed to discuss capacity, but María had shut the topic down. It was great to grow and expand, but our latest venture was still too new to know if it was short-term growth or if we could expect it to last more than one season.

But María was right. Our shop was small for all the business we currently generated, and there was nowhere to expand our current place. We had tenants on either side of our shop, and a few empty storefronts were available for rent in Northport, but they were either too small or too run down.

"Why don't we move some of our front stuff out that's taking up space and focus on the meats?" I asked.

"Because selling seasonings and other essentials makes our meat sell faster. Not to mention those have a higher profit margin," María said.

"But what do we make more money on, the cooked foods or the butchered meats?" I asked.

María sighed. "We all know the answer to that question, Manuel. But are we willing to throw caution to the wind? Are we willing to become a restaurant and give up the butcher shop? How long will our capacity last? We have all these cows, and selling them at market value, as you've said time and time again, would put us in the red. We only make money because we sell directly to the customer."

"So, we need a different place."

She shrugged. "It's not like the building we're leasing is all that nice. We're in one of the least busy parts of Northport. We're only there because Mr. Lancaster knew the previous owner. I think we should start looking for a more desirable location to sell our meats *and* the restaurant-style foods."

We tabled the discussion after that, but María had already given us a lot to consider. That night I stared at my bedroom ceiling and wondered how the world had shifted so quickly. Just a few weeks ago, I called our father, asking him to help me figure out how to tell my siblings we were about to lose everything. Now we were going to look for a place to expand. And all that success led back to one individual, a man I longed for and would never have. It was almost enough to drive me to drink.

I couldn't sleep, so I drove around the pastures, more to deal with a restless feeling than any issues on the farm. Inevitably, I ended up at the farmstead. Rhys, Justin's contractor, had almost finished with the property renovation. It already looked like a different place. The new paint and shiny metal roof made me think of the beautiful homes they showed on the renovation TV shows.

The place complemented Justin. For a moment, I indulged myself as I thought about what it would be like to live there with him, but I quickly shook off the fantasy. It was not to be, no matter how much I might want it.

Justin

UNCLE JEFF put his foot down about Sunday. "You're always with your new business partners, and we *are* proud of you and for you, but *we* are still your family. You need to spend Sunday with us."

I laughed and hugged him as I agreed. "Okay, what's the plan?" I asked, and when they told me we were going to a new food truck in Wilcox, I was excited. I'd heard good things about it.

As we drove to where the truck was parked, across from the town hall, I looked at the old Bellingham's Grocery and noticed it was closed and appeared empty. "What's going on with Bellingham's?" I asked, confused. The only other grocery store in the area was in Northport, a decent drive from here. I remembered Bellingham's always being packed with customers.

"Oh, that's a sad story," Uncle Henry said. "The family tried to keep that place running, but it was impossible. Once Mrs. Bellingham went into the hospital with a broken hip, they tried to sell but couldn't get a buyer. Then, after the old gal passed away, the family sold all the groceries and closed up shop."

"Do you mind if we pull over so I can take a peek inside?"

"Why do you want to see inside?" Uncle Henry asked.

"I might know a buyer or tenant."

"Well, you're in luck. I'm still the family's attorney, so I'm the one that keeps the keys. Let's go—"

"No, we can't go," Uncle Jeff argued. "Tonight we're going to have a nice dinner. You two can crawl around in that dusty old building tomorrow."

Uncle Henry winked at me in the rearview mirror, and I had to force the smile down. I had been working nonstop, either at the shop or at home. Uncle Jeff wasn't wrong. It'd been too long since we'd spent time together as a family.

I had to force myself not to say something about family dinners with Manuel's family. I still didn't know them well enough to bring my family over, but maybe one day I could merge the two.

I could see Bellingham's from the food truck and had to force myself not to look. Finally, after we finished eating, Uncle Jeff stood, grabbed our trash, and stared at us both for a moment. "Go on and ask Henry your questions. I know you're dying to. Then, if you want, the two of you can crawl around the building while I go shoot the breeze with Jonah," he said, pointing at the house where Jonah Beckham had lived as long as I could remember.

I jumped up and hugged him. "Thanks, Uncle Jeff. Can we?" I asked Uncle Henry, and he laughed and stood.

Sure, I don't see why not. I moved my new office in with Tim and his new guy, Jason. Do you remember Tim? He's been an attorney here for years."

I nodded. "Yes, he's the mayor's husband." Uncle Henry had always been friendly with him, and even though Uncle Henry worked in Northport, the county seat, he would sometimes chat with Tim when we were in Wilcox. I'd also met him again the night of the party, when Polly and Declan asked if we could cater three weddings.

We'd catered those three weddings one weekend after the other, and all three had rave reviews from Declan and Pierce. Of course, it was ridiculously hard to get the meats ready when we had customers we were turning away from the butcher shop.

By the time we got to the former grocery store, the sun was beginning to set, so I didn't have time to walk around the outside of the building, but I could do that tomorrow.

Inside, the shelves, freezers, and refrigerators all stood in the same places I remembered from years ago. The lime-green walls of my childhood had been painted a cheerful yellow, and the cracked old floor tiles now had what appeared to be reinforced linoleum. It looked so much better than when I was young.

"Wow, this is in excellent condition. Why didn't anyone buy it?"

"Small town, low profit margins in grocery. I'm sure it's also quite a lot to handle."

I nodded, thinking that had to be true. "What are they asking for it?"

When Uncle Henry told me, my initial excitement dimmed. "Wow, that's a lot of money."

He shrugged. "It's also in a prime location here in town and comes with good parking. If you know of a business that wants to expand and is willing to do so in Wilcox, I know the Bellingham family would be open to rent or maybe even owner finance. Keep in mind that the building that houses the post office goes with the grocery store, and the postal contract will fall on whoever takes this over, as will the income from the rent."

My uncle had given me a lot to think about, but I also needed more information. I didn't want to present my idea to anyone until I was sure it was feasible. "Uncle Henry, who would I speak to about getting groceries delivered? I don't know anything about operating a grocery store."

"Well, if you're serious, I can probably help, but if you really want someone to chase down those details, that'd be your uncle Jeff."

I grinned. Uncle Jeff was like a dog with a bone regarding research. The years he worked as an investigator for a Eugene-based law firm had also honed those skills. "Okay, well, I'll bring it up on the way home. Just so you're warned."

"Not a problem," he said, smiling, and I thought Uncle Henry might be setting something up. Uncle Jeff had retired a few years ago, and I wondered if maybe he had too much time on his hands. He'd spent so much time with me while I was going through the grieving process that I knew for a fact he was a little stir-crazy. There were only so many puzzles a person could put together.

As we drove home, I explained to my uncles the dilemma of how the butcher shop was nowhere near big enough to meet the demands of our clientele.

"If you move into Bellingham's, will you still have the same customer base?" Uncle Jeff asked.

"Yeah. I recognize at least half of the customers from growing up in Wilcox. Northport is half an hour away, but folks here have to travel there for groceries anyway, and that goes both ways. If we could keep the crowds happy by continuing to make great food and more of it, people would seek us out wherever we are."

"We're closer to Eugene than Northport is," Uncle Henry added. "You said last week that several people drove all the way from there for your brisket on word of mouth alone. It's possible you could increase your tourist traffic too."

"So, Uncle Jeff, I'm not good at research, but I don't want to present this idea to the Lópezes until I've had time to get numbers together, including what it's going to take to stock the shelves."

Uncle Jeff pondered a moment. "Justin, I'll help, but neither you nor your uncle are that clever. I know what you're up to, and I don't need you two babysitting me. So I need to say this before I do anything. If word gets out that you're looking to reopen the hometown grocery store, there's going to be a lot of hopeful people. It's tough for a small town to operate when such an anchor is lost."

"If this is feasible, we may need to do a fundraiser. I... well, I can't speak for the López family, but I'm concerned it would be too much. I certainly don't have the resources to open by myself, let alone keep it running."

While Uncle Henry drove, Uncle Jeff turned toward the back seat to face me, and I could tell the wheels were moving in his mind. "Why don't you give me a few days to put together a plan? In fact, you can bring barbecue home Friday night. I'll have something to share with you then."

I reached over the seat and hugged my uncle. "Thanks. You don't know how much this means to me."

Uncle Jeff patted my shoulder. "Son, seeing you find life again after... well, it's worth whatever it takes to see you happy. Besides, it gives me something to do other than harass your Uncle Henry."

Uncle Henry groaned, then winked at me in the rearview mirror. Yeah, he'd set all this up. The man was a master at making things go his way, especially when it actually benefited all of us.

That night I fell asleep thinking how lucky I'd been to have these two men as my family, my role models. If anyone could figure out how to make my store idea work, it'd be my uncle Jeff.

Manuel

MY WEEK started busy and just got worse. A herd of elk broke through one of my fences on Justin's property, which meant half our cattle herd got out onto National Forest land, and none of us could afford the fine if we didn't get them back quickly.

The only thing that saved us was Mr. Fitzgibbons. He rented the land from the National Forest and had been friends with Mr. Lancaster, so he called when he saw our brand mixed with his.

It took a whole day to round up the cattle and separate ours from his and another day to repair the fencing. Those elk had done quite a number on them. It was so bad I dreamed of venison, even though I wasn't much of a hunter. This year might be the exception.

Luckily none of our heifers or cows were in heat, so we avoided another mutt calf catastrophe. If we weren't still dealing with a drought, I'd pull the cattle into our pastures.

Not much more I could do about that than pray for rain. Maybe it was time to do that too, although the last time I'd seen a priest, he spent over an hour telling me how being gay would lead straight to hell. I told María and Carlos what the priest had said, and although both were very religious people, neither had set foot in church since then. That's not what I wanted, faith is an important thing, but I was happy they supported me no matter what.

I caught sight of Justin a few times, but even if I weren't avoiding him, I didn't have time to do anything other than look in his direction. Well, until Thursday. I'd gone to check on the newly repaired fence to make sure the elk hadn't torn it down again when I swung around to check on the little cattle herd that tended to shelter in the valley.

It was strange for cattle to split into groups, but for some reason, this bunch kept away from the main herd. We'd seen bears and cougars in the area lately, so it was best to keep a close eye on all the livestock. That went double for the splinter group, since it included the three new moms and their calves.

Threats to our livelihood notwithstanding, I always enjoyed having an excuse to visit the peaceful valley. On this side of the mountain, the land sloped toward where the little stream met the river that wound through Wilcox. It was secluded, though not far off the main road.

I'd just rounded a bend when I spotted someone jump into the water. "Pinches morros," I muttered as I parked the ATV. I couldn't get it down the hill from here, so I headed down on foot. We couldn't afford a bunch of wild teenagers antagonizing the heifers and calves. Nor could we afford anyone getting injured while trespassing on private property.

I trudged into the clearing just in time for Justin to pop out of the water. Completely, utterly, bare-assed naked. And mother of God, what an ass.

If not for the mooing in the distance, I could've sworn time stopped as I drank in the sight. Well, until he spotted me and I started falling all over myself.

"I, um, thought you… weren't *you*."

Justin quickly ducked his torso back under the water, but he was smiling. "I couldn't resist taking a dip to cool off. Wanna join me?" he asked.

Damn, I wanted to. But there would be no hiding the hard-on I was now sporting if I were to get naked or even just strip to my undies. Still, that didn't mean I wouldn't fantasize about it for the rest of my life.

"Um, no, I should go," I said, feeling my cheeks burning. "The cows need tending. Sorry to disturb you."

"Manuel, wait," Justin said as he crawled out of the water. I had the decency to look away this time, though only after catching another glimpse of his cute and very white butt glowing in the afternoon sun. He quickly pulled his shorts on—no underwear—and a shirt.

"So, I know you've been avoiding me, and you know… I-I was hoping we could talk."

Maybe now you have clothes on, I thought, which my brain took as permission to detour to visions of a wet, glistening Justin and his long cock. Nope, a conversation wasn't possible right now. "I need to go," I said and turned to head back up the hill where I'd left the ATV.

To my surprise, Justin reached out a hand to stop me. More excuses to get away died on my tongue when I saw the same hunger I felt reflected in his expression.

"Listen, we're in a precarious position," he said, but he didn't remove his hand from my arm. "I-I've been thinking a lot about us, about our situation." He turned, walked over to a large boulder, sat down, and patted it to get me to sit next to him. "I loved Donny, my boyfriend. I will always love him. He always wanted the best for me, and I know he still does, even if it's a life without him."

I didn't know what to say to that, so I remained silent. I'd be damned if I closed the door on this man by sticking my foot in my mouth.

Then Justin turned to me and made eye contact. "My father never got over losing my mother, and that grief became all-consuming after my grandparents died. Nothing and no one mattered to him anymore, least of all me, to the point that his self-destruction nearly destroyed us both." He let out a shaky breath. "I don't want to become him, Manuel. I'm afraid if I'm not honest with myself about what I want and don't start living my life again, that's exactly what will happen."

Was he saying what I thought he was saying? "And what exactly is it you want, Justin? Me? I mean, like, us?" I asked, waving my finger between us.

He nodded, looking relieved I hadn't tried to bolt again. "If you want to try, I'm willing. I just… it has to be slow. And I don't want your family or mine to know about it, at least not at first. I have a feeling if they get involved, they'd prop us in front of an altar inside of two seconds."

That made me chuckle because he had my family's number. My sisters-in-law, especially, had been trying to fix me up with someone—anyone, really—since we arrived in Oregon. María started long before that even.

I still had some lingering reservations about mixing business with pleasure, but Justin had a point. Why deny myself, and him, a shot at a loving relationship when tomorrow wasn't guaranteed? He knew that better than anyone.

"So, going slow. What does that mean?"

Justin smiled, leaned toward me, and gently kissed my lips. "It means just that—getting to know each other at that pace. Then, if we both want to pursue more, we can move things to the next level."

I don't think I'd moved so quickly in all my life. I stood and pulled him off the boulder and into my arms. His surprised laugh was cut off with another kiss. Only this time there was nothing gentle about it. I wanted this man more than I could say. To hell with the alarm bells going off in my brain about being in business together and him being our landlord. I no longer cared about anything other than the here and now—holding him, kissing him, loving him… although maybe it was too soon for that.

When Justin pulled back, I could see a glimmer of sadness in his eyes and took that as a sign he wasn't ready for more right then. So, as much as it hurt me to do so, I stepped back and lifted his hand to my mouth. "Thank you for being so open and honest with me. We will go slow, as slow as you need. But, *mi amor*, I know what my heart wants. When you're ready, I will give you the world."

Justin's face registered shock, and when his cheeks pinked to crimson, I smiled. I still had what it took to cause a handsome man to swoon. I kissed the back of his hand while looking into his eyes, and then I turned and headed back up the slope to my ATV. He'd finally opened the door, and I was going to woo him with all I had in me.

Justin

I'D SPENT every evening this week working with Uncle Jeff on the grocery-store idea. The more I learned, the more I became convinced that buying and reopening it was the best option—for me, for the López family, and for Wilcox.

Much of a grocery store's expense was sourcing fresh meat, but I had that resource right in my pocket. And with the money left over from Donny's life insurance policy, I could put down a hefty down payment.

The same truck that'd delivered groceries to Bellingham's for decades could do the same for us. One call to the Bellingham family was all it took to get the needed contacts. Luckily—and this really was luck—the grocery supplier for this area was a national company with good discounted merchandise. Overall, the entire venture seemed manageable.

While I worked closely with Uncle Jeff, he spent the time prodding me about life. He wasn't the nagging type. He was more subtle than that. In fact, he was pretty gifted at helping me understand that life only gave you so many chances. Reject enough and they eventually stop coming.

With that revelation came a torrent of thoughts about Manuel López. I liked him. There was no way around that. I loved Donny, I liked Manuel, and it was time for me to stop comparing the two. But was that even possible? I wasn't sure, but I knew I wouldn't find out unless I stopped pushing Manuel away.

Of course, the universe quickly responded after I had that epiphany. On Monday I helped Rhys do what he called a spot check of the farmhouse renovation, and then he and his crew spent the next couple of days finishing up. He called Wednesday to say he was ready to surrender the keys. So, the house was done. Finally, *finally*, done.

I'd avoided Wilcox my entire adult life, but Iowa had never felt like home. It was too flat, and Donny's family, except for his sister Margaret, hated me. Donny had been my home—not the farm, not his family, not the community.

All that had changed since I arrived back to Oregon, largely thanks to the López family. They were a part of me now, and my soul healed and grew as I spent more and more time with them. I'd even grown closer to Uncle Jeff and Uncle Henry, which surprised me since we'd always been tight-knit. But the biggest surprise was how I was beginning to care about so many other folks I'd met in Wilcox. I'd formed the kind of real friendships I'd craved and desperately needed as a kid growing up here. I adored Dalton and Pierce and their niece and nephew. Although I didn't get to spend much time with them since they were always in school or spending time with one of Dalton's relatives.

Rhys and Xander were hilarious when they weren't working, and I'd already met them a couple of times at Levi's parents' farm, where Cliff took me on a very detailed tour of his and Chris's aquaponics operation. Levi and his wife had a new baby girl, and I rarely saw them, but I had a feeling that, as things calmed down for them, I'd begin to develop relationships there as well.

Northport still wasn't my favorite place, but it never had been. Not just because it was our rival town, but because it wasn't as friendly as Wilcox. Sure, we had pleasant customers at the butcher shop, but the whole vibe of the area was different. That, and the shop wasn't in a prime location.

I'd already decided to present the relocation proposal to the López family on Sunday, at their weekly family dinner. Uncle Jeff was putting together a formal pro forma, as he called it, for me to give to them. He'd become intrigued by my ownership now that we'd seen that the profit margins worked.

But first I needed to have an honest conversation with Manuel. I felt like we'd been walking on eggshells around each other for weeks, and that's when he *hadn't* been outright avoiding me. I'd have to get him alone to speak, but his very nosy family wouldn't let any conversation around them be private. That just wasn't their way. So when I came up for air after jumping into the secluded stream for a skinny-dip, I almost laughed when I saw him staring.

I'd had to quickly submerge myself because my cock took notice of the way he was eyeing my junk. Despite my body's eager response, I didn't want our first conversation in ages to lead to sex.

It had felt good talking to him and finally getting my pent-up feelings off my chest. When I kissed him, it's like sparks lit up in my head. I wanted him so badly, but when he kissed me back, the guilt and worry returned. Thankfully, he agreed to take it slow, then kissed my hand and called me mi amor. And holy fuck, I could've melted right there on the spot.

I walked back to the house in a bit of a daze, replaying Manuel's romantic gesture in my mind. I felt like he'd given me a gift simply by being himself. Not only was he interested and willing to give me space, he understood I needed us to take things at my pace. I couldn't ask for more than that from a potential partner.

The farmhouse smelled and looked like a new home inside. I no longer saw nostalgic or haunting reminders of my grandparents or my father. Instead I saw potential. I saw my future—one that might even include Manuel.

Even I thought it ridiculous to be picturing him settled into my newly remodeled home—a guy I'd only just kissed for the first time— but the vision came so easily. I saw Sunday dinners with our combined families in the open-concept dining room, gatherings on the wide front porch with family and friends after a barbecue cookout, Manuel and me stripped down and playing underwater grab-ass at the swimming hole.

Somehow I knew, maybe in my head more than my heart, that Donny was okay with that. He'd loved me and would want me to be happy. And in the most unlikely turn of events, my happiness was now firmly rooted in family, friends, and Wilcox, Oregon. Along with the sweet and handsome cattle farmer who lived nearby.

As I left the house and climbed into my recently purchased older-model pickup, I felt warmth flow around me. For a brief second, it felt like Donny was there, and with that came the pang of loss. That's what they say about grief, that it can hit you full force out of nowhere. But behind the familiar feeling bloomed something else, something that nearly tore a sob from my throat—understanding.

On more than one occasion, Donny had mentioned how sad he was that my father had hurt me—physically and emotionally. He also regretted his family had treated me so poorly. They loved and supported him, but for whatever reason, that ended when they met me. He must've known I'd never be able to stay in that environment, unsupported and disliked, if anything happened to him.

As the warmth subsided, I realized he, of all people, would understand this was my chance to escape that reality. Tears rolled down my face as something in the distance caught my eye. I glanced up at the mountainside that led to the López's place and saw Manuel's ATV bouncing across the pasture toward their home.

In that moment, I would forever believe Donny had given me his blessing to love again.

Manuel

I WAS SINGING when I climbed out of the shower and dried off. I still enjoyed the old love songs of Mexico, and I could carry a tune well enough. If life had gone a different way and I had stayed closer to my roots, I would've loved to have joined a maríachi band.

There was little need for such things in the hills of Oregon, but that didn't mean I didn't belt the songs out as I thought of my undeniably sexy neighbor. And landlord. And business partner. And, though perhaps too soon to say, boyfriend.

I sprayed on just a little cologne because it made me feel good about myself. Too much and my family would give me shit about it. If I were going to keep Justin and me a secret, I couldn't be showing too many signs of love. They were all too attuned to me for that.

I went to my closet and cringed. I had nothing to wear but beaten-up blue jeans and worn-out shirts. Even my nicer clothes were sporting some holes. When had my entire life become about the farm? I couldn't woo a man looking like I'd just come in from a barn.

I knew I had too much to do to be running off like a love-sick teenager, but there were priorities to be managed. I could stop by the shop and check on María, Cassie, and Justin. Maybe, since he was on summer break, I could steal my nephew. He had better taste in clothes than I did, but he would totally tell on me to his mother.

I could always threaten him that if he blabbed, I'd return the favor. That tended to keep Antonio's big mouth under control. The thought made me chuckle.

I had to search for the radio station that played my favorite love songs, then turned it up loud and sang along as I drove to Northport. I almost parked in front of the butcher shop, but quickly realized I'd get caught up in the shop's drama if I did. Hell, it was afternoon, and the line still wound around the corner. Yeah, there would be no shopping if I went in there.

So I drove around the corner to the old Western store. Mostly they sold boots, but I'd found some nice shirts and jeans last time I looked.

People these days tend to buy stuff online or at the big stores, but I preferred small local shops, even though that probably meant I was old-fashioned.

I walked in and smiled at the same old woman who'd staffed the store last time I visited. Was that a year ago? Two? She smiled and nodded.

I found the shirts, and a wave of happiness came over me. I loved the old Western styles, even if they were a bit gaudy for today's tastes. They made me stick out as a cowboy, but then, I suppose I was one.

I hummed "Hermosa Cariño" as I grabbed three new shirts, and was thankful I'd kept an account separate from my family.

I knew I needed at least another good pair of jeans, so I grabbed ones I knew would fit and was about to check out when the most beautiful pair of black boots sparkled at me. The clothes were necessary, but it'd be stupid to blow money on boots, especially since we were only beginning to dig out of our financial slump.

I forced myself to walk away, but the image of Justin's beautiful body came to mind. A man like him deserved to be wooed by a gentleman, not some cowpoke with cow shit smeared on his boots. *Screw it*, I thought, and found the boots in my size and sat to try them on.

They fit perfectly. I had to resist the urge to spin around in them, but I knew they'd be the perfect boots for dancing. Maybe some two-stepping and line dancing, but that wasn't what I had in mind. I wanted to feel Justin pressed up against me. I wanted him to sway in my arms as I pulled him close for a slow dance.

The thought had me swallowing hard and moving slightly to adjust my jeans. I was definitely buying these boots, even if I had to deal with my guilt later.

I took everything to the register, and the lady checked me out, but she paused when she got to the turquoise shirt. She placed it next to the boots and, without saying anything, reached over to take a beautiful belt buckle out of the display to her right. "You'll need this to go with the outfit," she said, and I wanted to argue, but she was right. It was made of black stone that I assumed was obsidian, and the turquoise beads woven around it matched the shirt perfectly.

I nodded but frowned when she slipped the boxed buckle into my shopping bag without ringing it up. "Ma'am, don't I need to pay for that?" I asked.

She smiled. "Señor López," she said, surprising me that she remembered my name, "these are courting clothes. A woman my age knows such things. This is my gift for love, and since I own this store, I can do as I please. Consider this a good luck charm to you and your beloved."

I expected her to say "woman" or "lady friend," but when she didn't, I smiled and accepted the kind gift. I paid, thanked her, and took my new *courting* outfit to my truck.

That solved one problem, but I still had one more—where to take Justin for our first date. Again I avoided the butcher shop and drove over to the Wilcox Community Center. The two little towns were just far enough apart that the daily gossip mill here might be a little slower to reach my sisters-in-law than in Northport.

I couldn't guarantee the lady at the Western store wouldn't go blabbing to María or Cassie, given she must know my family ran the butcher shop near her store, but I could ignore that. If they found out what I was doing next, it would be harder to explain away than buying new clothes.

I walked into the center and found the person I was looking for. "Hello, Mr. Smith," I said as I approached the desk.

"Hello, Manuel. What brings you in today? I haven't seen you in a month of Sundays."

I smiled at the old man. It had been a long time. "I, well, I was wondering, are you still holding community dances here on Friday nights?" I asked.

"The one where we serve dinner first?" he asked, and I nodded. "We are, but only once a month now. Interest dies down until fall. Why, you got yourself a new sweetheart?"

I shrugged noncommittally and fought the urge to nod. "Maybe, or at least planning on trying." Then I paused, unsure how to ask my next question. Finally I just blurted, "You were open to gay couples attending before. Is that still the case?"

Mr. Smith's expression morphed from curious to kind. "Manuel, Wilcox is a safe place. Of course you and yours will be welcome, and in fact, you will be one of many who show up. Our dances are open to everyone, even those with two left feet."

I chuckled at that and sighed with relief. "Okay, thanks, sir. Do I need to RSVP or anything?"

"Oh yeah, you should. That's how we know how much food to cater. Speaking of, I hear you and your family are doing quite the barbecue spread these days. If you ever want to cater one of our events, just let me know. We're always looking for something new to share, especially local fare."

I nodded and was genuinely grateful, but right then I didn't want to mix business with my dating life. So I simply thanked him and told him I'd RSVP as soon as I knew when we'd be coming. He gave me a schedule, and I stuffed it into my pocket. There was a dance this weekend, and I really would enjoy that being our first date.

I was about to head to Justin's house to ask him out when I saw the man himself standing in front of an empty building. He was talking to some man I didn't know. A good-looking man—tall with broad shoulders.

Disappointment and a flash of jealousy struck me at seeing Justin with another guy. But before I had a chance to make a fool of myself, the man reached out and shook Justin's hand. That was even more puzzling. Had they been talking business? What kind of business was Justin doing in Wilcox?

That led me to wonder if he was leaving the butcher shop. If that was the case, I needed to know sooner rather than later. I rushed across the street and called Justin's name just as he was about to climb into his truck.

"Hey," he said, looking surprised and a little guilty. "Fancy seeing you here in town."

"Same. So, who was that guy?" I asked, trying not to sound suspicious.

For a few seconds, he stood silently, looking at his feet. "Well, shit, I wasn't planning on telling you yet, but you'd find out soon enough anyway," he said, meeting my eyes. "I've taken a contract on the old grocery store."

"What?" I asked, caught completely off-guard. I looked up at the empty building and then back at him. "You took a contract, like, you're buying it?"

Justin shrugged. "Maybe, but only if I can convince María and the rest of your family this is the place to expand."

Relief washed over me and was immediately replaced with annoyance. "This is for our business? Why haven't you mentioned it?"

"Well, I would've, but I needed to make sure it made sense first. There was a lot to consider, and you weren't really up for discussing it at the time, so I didn't want to mention anything until I had a strong grasp on whether it was even feasible."

I looked at him for a few beats and then shook my head. "Justin, this is too much. We're still struggling—"

"I know," he interrupted, "but have you been to the shop lately? The lines get longer by the day. I-I remember this old grocery store fondly, and Uncle Jeff says since it closed, it's been a sore spot for the town, having to drive to Northport just for groceries."

I didn't know what to say. I was upset, but probably not for any good reason. Normally I would walk away, but I didn't want to risk making the situation worse or make him mad, not when we were just getting to the point where he considered me more than a business partner.

Justin must've sensed my unease because he grabbed my hand. "Hey, come in. I'll show you what I have in mind, and if you want, we can go over the numbers Uncle Jeff helped me draw up. That way, you can help me discuss it with your family."

I followed him inside, noting that he had a key. "So, as you can see," he said, pointing at the shelves, "it's set up and ready to be used again. The woman's family who owned the grocery closed it when she passed away, and her family has been trying to sell it, but so far, no one has come forward."

If no one wanted it, didn't that confirm it was a money pit? I glanced around and nodded at Justin to continue the tour.

"I'd recommend we resurrect this as a grocery store. I was at a butcher shop in Iowa that also sold groceries, and it was really successful. We could do something like that here," he said, walking around the checkout counter and toward the cold storage. "Owen, that's the man I was talking to? He's one of the owners. He said all the freezers are relatively new and were replaced within the last ten years. All of them work—I've checked—and they hold the right temperatures, even though they've been empty for a year."

He led me to the back of the building then and showed me a tiny section for the butcher shop. "This is the only thing that doesn't work as-is. Bellingham's didn't sell much fresh meat, which, obviously, wouldn't be the case for us. Running the numbers, it's clear the butcher shop is what would keep the rest of the grocery store solvent and profitable."

I followed him through a back door and into a dark enclosed space. "This was all storage, and I think it just became a place to toss crap they didn't know what to do with. However, in the seventies, it was a sandwich shop. When it closed, they just boarded up the wall. There's electricity," he said, pointing at several outlets on the floor, "for all our meat displays. I'd recommend using this entire space for the butcher shop. And since it has its own door, we could install a counter and wait on customers from both sides. People could eat in here too, sorta like having a restaurant inside the grocery store."

Justin's enthusiasm built the longer he talked. It was evident he and his uncle had put a lot of thought into the venture. "So people can walk in and buy from the butcher shop without going into the grocery store? Or shop at the butcher shop from the grocery store?"

He winked at me. "Exactly, and sit down for some brisket besides. I don't have the spreadsheet with me, but if we're even half as successful as we are in Northport, we will bring in a considerable profit. And Bellingham's wasn't doing a horrible business when it closed. The family just couldn't run the place and couldn't find a buyer."

"Even if the old grocery was doing all right and we could replicate that, we'd need to turn a solid profit to justify moving operations here. Why would our business be so much more profitable than theirs?" I asked.

Justin lifted his arms into the air as if the space we were in were already the butcher shop. "Meat. Bellingham's only had that tiny meat section in the back because it was killing them financially. Remove that cost from the equation and the grocery store's profits rise about ten to fifteen percent. We already have a butcher shop and supply all the beef ourselves, so comparing their business model to ours is a bit apples versus oranges."

The numbers bounced around inside my head. "Justin, it's a lot to consider. Do you really think it would work?"

"Yeah, and more importantly, it's drought-proof." Justin took my hands in his, and I looked at him, surprised. "Listen, María and Cassie told me about what you all went through, not knowing what to do with the cows and with hay prices and low sales at the market. With this place, we could sell meat at a discount. Owen told me Bellingham's used to have meat sales, and even though they didn't usually earn much from the meat, they turned a nice profit because they sold so much of it. Anyway, I think this could solve a lot of our problems. It could also help the town."

I looked at him for a long moment, then down at our joined hands. "Why is this important to you?" I asked, feeling just a little guilty. Obviously he was in business with my family now, but I needed to know what was driving him personally.

Justin pulled his hands back, walked toward the front of the building, and paused for me to catch up. "Manuel, I've never felt like I belonged, not really. My dad was a bad man, and I didn't have many friends growing up. I felt like an outsider in my own hometown. Then I went to college in another small town and had very little in common with anyone there. Sure, I had a boyfriend, but Donny's family hated me. I think they just hated he was gay, and I embodied that for them."

He leaned back against the checkout counter, and I did the same. "I feel like I belong with your family—María, Cassie, your brothers, even your nephew. They already feel like close friends, if not family. I-I want to be a part of that, for them." He looked down and studied the floor, then in a quiet voice added, "For you."

My heart melted, and I reached out to draw him into my arms. "Mi amor, you don't have to do anything for us to love you. We already think of you as family." I lifted his chin so he could look at me and gently kissed his sweet mouth. "This looks like it might be a good idea, though. I'm impressed. Shocked, but impressed."

Justin smiled. "So you like my idea?"

I nodded. "I want to see all the numbers before I cast a vote, and then you need to have my papá look them over, because he's amazing at figuring out problems before they occur. But yeah, I think it's a good plan."

Justin leaned into me and pressed his lips to mine, but he wasn't gentle. It was the kiss of a man who'd been seen and understood. I took all he had to give and gave it back, deepening the kiss and showing him how much he was cared for.

When the chime above the front door sounded, we pulled back and turned to see Justin's uncle Henry smiling like he'd just won the lottery. "Well, sorry to interrupt, boys, but I saw the door was cracked open and wanted to check on the place."

Justin chuckled, sounding embarrassed, but didn't pull away. "You've got perfect timing, Uncle Henry," he said. "I was just showing the place to Manuel."

"Yeah, showing the place, so that's what the kids are calling it these days," he said, and I snorted despite myself. I gave Justin a quick peck and released my hold. I had a hell of a lot of chores to get done, and the day wasn't getting any longer.

"Oh, I forgot, I was going to ask you to go to the dance with me Friday night. It's why I was here in town, to see if it was still happening. Would you like to go with me?"

Justin's adorable face blushed, and when he looked at his uncle, I realized I'd just asked him out in front of him. In my defense, Henry had walked in on us enjoying a passionate kiss. Asking Justin to go dancing seemed tame by comparison.

"I… yeah, I'd like that," he said.

"Great. Should I pick you up at your uncles' place or your farmhouse?"

"Seeing as I haven't moved into the house yet, best be at the uncles'."

I couldn't resist and gave him a kiss on the cheek. "See you Friday night, then. I'll be there at five."

I walked past Henry and got a pat on the back with a quiet "Good job."

I *had* done a good job wooing, but the grocery store business still had me worried. That was a lot to take on—more than I was sure we should—but Justin had made a lot of good points. I looked forward to hearing him lay it all out to the family, and if I had anything to say about it, that would happen on Sunday.

I had no doubt every family member would make their opinions known, and rightly so. This was a major decision that would impact all of us, including Justin, and we all had to be on board. If it wasn't going to work out, I didn't want him blowing money on it just because he thought he needed to in order for us to want him. I already wanted him, and I knew for a fact my family loved him like our own.

For now I'd let him present his idea and support him in doing so. Up until now everything he'd proposed had become a success. And even though it was very early days, I liked to think that winning streak even included the two of us.

Justin

"So, you've had a change of heart," Uncle Henry said, and I shook my head.

"Don't start," I said, and he laughed out loud.

"I'm not starting anything, but last time we talked, you were set against getting involved. Is this a fling or something serious?"

I sighed as I looked toward the front door Manuel had just exited through. "Uncle Henry, it's something I don't understand. I mean, it's mixed up with a lot of emotions."

"I bet. Let's lock up, walk over to the café, and you can explain."

I wasn't getting out of talking no matter how much I wanted to. When I moved in with Uncle Henry and Uncle Jeff, I'd been so hurt, so distraught, that all I wanted to do was hide. But they wouldn't hear of it. They kept drawing me out, over and over, until I was able to trust humanity again. As hard as that was, I loved them for it.

Once inside the café, I rushed to the bathroom, as much to give myself a moment to think as to wash my hands after being in the dusty old building. When I came out, Uncle Henry had a large piece of apple pie with two scoops of ice cream sitting in front of him.

Our local café sucked so bad when it came to meals, but they made some of the best pies I'd ever eaten.

I laughed as I sat down and he handed me a spoon. "You think this is an apple pie à la mode kind of conversation?"

He smiled and took a bite, which was another of my uncle's tactics to get me to talk.

"So," he said a moment later, "tell me about all these emotions."

I sighed, took a huge bite of pie and ice cream, and chewed as I thought about where to start. "My dad. I think he's what caused me to change my mind. I've been thinking about how he acted and kept everyone at a distance. I realize now it was because he lost Mom and couldn't cope. I-I don't want to be like him."

Uncle Henry took my hand. "Justin, you're not your father. You aren't your mom either. You're different and more than them, in some ways. Your dad was an alcoholic before he married my sister. I talked with your grandfather about it before he died. They tried to get him into rehab, but he wasn't willing to change. You aren't an alcoholic, and you aren't unwilling to change."

I nodded, although it didn't dispel my concerns. "There's also the farmhouse. Rhys has completely finished the renovations, by the way. We did a walk-through, and it feels so new, so inviting. It doesn't even resemble the place I grew up in. That got me thinking about how I'm a lot like the old house—beaten down, abused, and on the verge of collapse—but with some time, effort, and care, I've been restored. A big part of that was because of you and Uncle Jeff, but also Donny. He loved me unconditionally." I swiped at a tear. "I think it's unusual for someone as damaged as I was to get someone like Donny to love them. I-I'm very lucky, even having lost him."

I sucked in a few sobs before they escaped, not wanting to make a spectacle of myself in the middle of town. My uncle gripped my hand more firmly in silent support as I blinked back additional tears.

"Uncle Henry," I was finally able to say, "I… what are the chances of finding that kind of love again? Manuel, he's special. Like one in a million, I think. I don't know him well, but he's always there to help his family. His nephew adores him. His brothers too, and their wives. My heart can't seem to let go of the thought of him. When I lost Donny, I thought that was it. Why wouldn't I? I mean, I'd lost the sun and the moon. Then my life changed and shifted, and suddenly, in the midst of the darkness, came such a bright ray of sunshine."

We sat there a moment until Uncle Henry pushed the pie toward me. I chuckled and scooped another spoonful into my mouth.

Uncle Henry smiled. "You may be *my* sister's son, but you are more like your uncle Jeff than me. You've overcome such horrors, but you've become beautiful people. I think you're lucky to have had Donny, but you don't recognize how lucky others are to have you. Do you feel guilty about caring for Manuel?"

I nodded. "I did at first. Then something changed when I saw the renovations. Well, that and a conversation I had with Uncle Jeff about Dad. I want to be like the old house—I want a chance to be restored like new, but

I also love the thought of having a stronger interior for having survived what I have. Does that even make sense?" I asked, and Uncle Henry nodded.

"Oh, son, it makes the best sense. Just so you know, Jeff and I discussed Manuel even before you came back home. He's solid, that one. Yes, he loves his family and will do whatever he has to for them, but he's got a good head on his shoulders. We understand why you'd be attracted to him and him to you. I didn't know Donny well—you lived too far away—but from what you've said about him, I think he would be proud that you've found love again."

I wiped away another tear and nodded, thinking about the incident in the truck when I felt like Donny had all but told me that himself.

"Okay, that's enough of that." I pulled the pie over to my side of the table and devoured the rest.

"Hey," Uncle Henry protested, but I shook my head.

"Nope, old man, if you're going to make me cry like a kid in public, I deserve all the pie. Fair is fair."

He laughed, waved to the server, and ordered himself a slice and one to take home to Uncle Jeff. I thought about that. I'd always known my uncles as a unit. I didn't differentiate Uncle Henry from Uncle Jeff just because one was blood-related and the other wasn't. They each seemed to love me and embody my family as much as the other.

Seeing Uncle Henry order pie for Uncle Jeff made me think about their relationship with each other too. They were so solid but always entrenched in love. I knew a bit about Uncle Jeff's upbringing and how he had overcome a lot. Uncle Henry had told me that was one of the reasons he was so protective of me—he wanted to save me from the horrors he encountered as a kid.

Other than that, his past didn't impact his relationship with his husband or me, which gave me hope. I think Uncle Henry was right. I wasn't my father. Losing myself to sorrow only hurt me and those who cared about me. Acceptance is supposed to be one of the stages of grief. Maybe acceptance that life goes on is a step beyond that.

I'd loved and lost, but now, by some strange, marvelous miracle, I felt ready to try and love again.

Manuel

I DECIDED TO forgo the farm and went to the butcher shop instead. It was almost five o'clock, an hour to closing, and we still had a line of people at the register. I went through the front and watched customers grab items. The shelves were virtually empty. The meats and our special spice blends were almost gone. I didn't visit the shop often, but I couldn't recall ever seeing it so bare.

I now got what Justin was saying. If we were even remotely as successful in Wilcox as here, the grocery store business would likely blow up in a good way.

I wandered out back to where Carlos was cutting up meat and Martín was putting it in trays to be stored in the refrigerators for tomorrow. Less than half a year ago, we were lucky to sell all the meat before it went bad. That accounted for all the meat we'd frozen. Now my brothers had to work full-time keeping the shelves stocked.

I thought of the old grocery store and the adjoining sandwich shop that'd been closed. The latter was the size of our butcher shop. That gave me an idea. If we opened a butcher shop in Wilcox first, we could test things out before actually relocating.

We'd have to have help, though. My mind immediately went to my parents, and I almost laughed out loud. We'd nearly talked Papá into moving a few times, despite his attachment to the El Paso house. Mamá had long ago said she'd come if he would, and I knew without a shadow of a doubt, if I told them we needed help setting up our new shop, they'd start packing. That's how we all operated—family first.

It was incredibly hard on my parents when my brothers and I moved away all at once, and I knew they still missed us desperately. They were too far away to continue watching Antonio, their only grandchild, grow up. But even if they agreed to pull up stakes, I still had to help Justin get the rest of the family on board with the plan.

I went to Carlos's office, opened the old desktop computer, and began to search for local meat lockers, display cases, and other items we'd need. We were operating at capacity here, so we couldn't take any equipment or supplies currently in use, but I didn't think we should invest in new stuff, not if we ended up moving to Wilcox permanently.

If we bought new, it would cost us over fifty thousand dollars to set up another butcher shop. I'd put away that much over the years, all of which I was prepared to give to my family to keep the business afloat, and if Justin was willing to invest in the idea, I could and would do the same. But I suspected that a little searching would turn up everything we'd need to open up for a fraction of what we'd spend buying new.

I printed off the equipment list, stapled it together, and deleted the browser history so my nosy brother wouldn't start asking questions—not before Justin could roll out his plans to everyone on Sunday. Now I just had to call my parents and convince them to come help.

It was going into hay season, and even though our hay wasn't going to be as good as it had been in previous years, my hands would soon be full again with farming. Antonio could help with the mowing, and maybe we could hire a few hands to help out elsewhere on the farm since I knew Martín and Carlos would be too busy at the shop, especially if they were prepping meat for two stores.

Yes, it could work, I thought as I drove home.

Luckily, the rain we'd finally had a couple of weeks ago had greened up the pastures, so I didn't need to worry about feeding hay right now. We'd also cut the herd down to a manageable size, even if we still had a significant surplus of steers compared to what we usually had this time of year.

So I figured I could get away with making my phone call to our parents instead of checking fences today. Fingers crossed, I wouldn't regret that.

I went to my room and shut the door, even though everyone was still at the butcher shop. I always felt better when I had private conversations in my room.

"Hey, Papá," I said when he answered.

"Hijo, are you okay?" he quickly asked. I supposed it was unusual for me to be calling before dark.

I told him I was fine. "Um, Papá, can you turn the phone on speaker? I need to talk to you and Mamá together."

I knew I was making him nervous, but it couldn't be helped. "Hola, hijo," Mamá said.

"Hola, Mamá. Necesito su ayuda," I pleaded for her help.

Justin

I WAS SO nervous when Manuel showed up at my uncles' to pick me up that I was physically shaking. "You okay?" Uncle Jeff asked.

"I'm fine, just, you know… got the jitters."

He smiled and came over to hug me. "Listen, this is a good thing, and Manuel is a sweet man. Enjoy the night, and if it gets to be too much, you can come home. Just call and we'll come get you if need be."

I smiled. I was well into my twenties, but my uncle sometimes still talked to me like I was that lost teenage boy. At one time that would've grated, but now it felt good knowing he cared.

"Thanks, Unc," I said as I hugged him back.

I walked to the main hallway, and when I knew neither of my uncles could see, I quickly checked myself in the hall mirror. I didn't make poor Manuel come to the door to fetch me. My uncles were overwhelming on the best of days, and with them knowing how nervous I was… I didn't want to expose my date to that.

When I saw his pickup pull into the driveway, I called out. "He's here. See you tonight or tomorrow morning," I said, blushing at the inference that I might not return tonight. I ran out of the house before either of my uncles could comment.

Manuel was dressed in new-looking Western wear, and damn if that didn't make him look even hotter than usual. "Hey," he said when I climbed into the truck.

"Hey," I replied, leaning over, not thinking about what I was doing. Manuel's eyes shot to mine; then he smiled and leaned in to meet me halfway. His work-roughened hand slid around the back of my head and pulled me in for a delicious kiss.

I moaned slightly at how good it felt to have his mouth on mine. Then he pulled away, leaving me unable to move.

"Ready to go?" he asked when I opened my eyes.

I nodded, leaned back, and snapped my seat belt into place.

"So, they have dinner. I checked, and it's Italian. I hope that's okay," he said, and I nodded again.

"It just feels good not to be stuck at home on a Friday night watching *The Golden Girls* reruns with my uncles. One can only handle so much horrible eighties fashion in one sitting."

"So you have low expectations for tonight?" he asked.

Before I could respond, he smiled. "I like *The Golden Girls*, but a night of dancing is good occasionally as well, no?"

"Yes, it's good," I replied, and I leaned back as Manuel drove us to the community center.

He met me as I slid out of his truck, took my hand, and led me inside the loud event.

As we walked in, I recognized several people. There would be quite a buzz through the grapevine tomorrow. I wasn't much to talk about these days, I'd been gone too long, but Manuel and his family were important people in the community.

Even though the butcher shop wasn't in Wilcox, folks here knew them, and more than a few townsfolk were customers and had told me how good the family was—honest, hardworking, kind people. I, of course, agreed wholeheartedly.

The food was self-service, so after paying, we filled our plates and found a table. I don't know why it felt so romantic—a buffet-style Italian spread and a table in the corner of the crowded community center.

I noticed there were quite a few couples, and people were milling around making small talk. It was a date night for folks. The thought made me smile as I sat across from Manuel.

"So, do you like to dance?" he asked me.

I shrugged. "I'm not very good at it. I mean, I took ballroom dance in college because I had to take a physical education class, but I don't know many line dances."

He dug into his food as he thought about what I'd said. "I grew up dancing to Mexican folk music. I even performed a few times at festivals in El Paso."

I grinned at that. "Maybe I can get one of those bright-colored dresses and be your partner sometime."

When his mouth opened and shut a few times, I leaned back and laughed. "You're easy to goad, Manuel. Honestly, I think that's pretty awesome. I haven't been to El Paso. Heck, I've not been to many places."

His eyes twinkled. "Maybe we should go when it's not quite as hot."

"Yes, I'd like that," I responded. Then I dug into my meal. When I swallowed, I said. "I'd like to meet your parents too."

When Manuel blushed, I wasn't sure if he was concerned about what my meeting them would be like or what it would mean for us from a relationship standpoint, so I dropped it. His brothers and their wives had embraced me wholeheartedly. Maybe his parents were more traditional.

I immediately thought of Donny's parents. Their dislike had been palpable. I forced myself to shake the thought out of my head—no need to ruin a wonderful evening.

"You okay?" Manuel asked, and I realized I must not have hidden my thoughts very well.

"Yeah," I said sadly. "Just sometimes, parents and relationships don't go hand in hand. I remember… sorry, I know I'm messing this up, but this is the first time I've been out on a date since Donny."

"Oh, you… you were thinking I meant my parents weren't open to me being gay?"

I nodded, and he smiled. "My mamá will love you. She's like María. She'll have too many questions and will embarrass me. Papá will shake your hand too hard and say, 'You have a good grip, good man.'" Manuel changed his voice to sound like his dad, which made me chuckle.

"Well, that's reassuring," I said. "They sound like good people, which doesn't surprise me, considering how well their sons turned out."

Manuel's blush returned, and I drank in the sight. "Speaking of my parents," he said, "I have a secret, but you can't tell María or the family. I want it to be a surprise."

"What?" I asked, confused but intrigued by his excitement.

"You're still planning to tell everyone about the grocery store idea on Sunday?" he asked, and I nodded. "Well, I think we should do a trial run of the butcher shop in Wilcox, and I asked Papá and Mamá to help set it up. We can't run both shops at the same time, not without help."

My eyes grew with the implication. "So you think they'll come? Move here, I mean?"

His smile said yes, but he shrugged. "Depends on what the family says on Sunday, but… maybe."

I reached for his hand across the table. "Manuel, that's amazing. But let's not talk about business tonight. We talk about that all the time. Tell me about your childhood and El Paso. It sounds wonderful."

Manuel's beautiful face bloomed at my request, and he regaled me with story after story about growing up in West Texas.

I could see it all in my mind—the desert and scrub brush, the home he grew up in, the loud extended family. It was overwhelming, considering how different his early life was compared to my own. I could tell he wanted to ask about my childhood, but he hesitated.

If he'd spoken to anyone around here, they'd have told him about my abusive father and how I'd had to go live with my uncles. Not that I hadn't already told him about some of that, but wanting to keep the good mood and reassure him that my entire life hadn't been awful, I launched into my best memories.

"Grandpa was all about his cows. When I was little, he'd let me tag along with him, and I loved watching the cows follow him around the pasture. Back then, he owned a huge four-wheeler that had to have been my dad's age. The cows would follow that thing single file like a bunch of elementary school kids." I smiled at the memories. "Grandma cooked, and even when I was too young to stand at the counter, she'd park me at the table and give me projects to help. I loved everything about the farm and my grandparents. Even my dad was a better person back then." I looked up and saw the sadness on Manuel's face. "I had a good childhood, Manuel. My teen years sucked, but my early years were filled with love and family. I-I think that's why I enjoy being around yours as much as I do. It reminds me of the good days on our farm."

Just then, the band began playing, and Manuel's smile returned. "Come on, I'll teach you how to do the slide," he said, and I laughed. Every human on the planet already knew how to do that one, so I assumed it wasn't difficult to learn.

We laughed and danced, surrounded by townsfolk. All of them enjoyed it as much as we did.

When the next song came on, he embraced me, two-stepping to the music. He just assumed I knew how, which, luckily, I did. We danced for a long time before the band slowed down and played a waltz.

I was about to walk off when Manuel caught my hand. "You said you did ballroom. Do you know how to dance to this?" he asked.

I nodded, and Manuel, who was slightly bigger than me, sidled up. He lifted our arms while his other hand slipped around my waist. I'd been following him since we started two-stepping, so it made sense for him to lead now.

He took me up, then back, as we began to step in time to the music, our bodies pressed together. His footwork was better than any of my classmates in school. I somehow knew how to anticipate his moves, and when he spun, I stepped into him, allowing our momentum to spin us before he stepped out and took me with him.

We were perfectly in tune, and my heart fluttered at how incredible it felt to be maneuvered around by this remarkable man—how it felt to let him lead me, move me, and guide me across the dance floor before throwing me out and then spinning me back to him.

I'd forgotten how much I loved to dance, and I'd never had a dance partner like Manuel—strong and commanding, yet gentle and graceful. When the song ended, he spun me, and we landed face-to-face just as the last note played. Breathing hard, I almost leaned in for a kiss when applause broke out.

Manuel and I blushed as we looked around the room. All eyes were on us, and folks clapped and whistled. Somehow, in the heat of that dance, we'd forgotten we were in public. Manuel waved and led me back toward the table. "Wanna wait for dessert, or shall we go somewhere, um, more private?" he asked quietly.

My blush from earlier deepened, but I didn't respond. Instead, I took his hand and pulled him out of the community center and toward his truck. As soon as we were inside, he looked at me. "I really like you," I said.

I didn't let him get the words out to respond before I dove in for a kiss—the one I'd meant to have after he'd waltzed with me. When I pulled back, I said, "Let's go to my house. I had a sofa delivered, so...."

He didn't need me to explain what I meant. Thank God I'd found that half-price sofa online. I hadn't thought much about furnishing the house, despite having chucked all of the old furniture. In any case, I wanted the privacy the place afforded us right now.

It took just under fifteen minutes to get from town to the old farmhouse. I found my key and let us in. The door shut just as Manuel's mouth found mine. He pushed me back against the closed door, his lips and tongue assaulting mine.

"God, I want you so bad," I said when we finally came up for air.

"You can have me," he said. Then he moved his lips to my neck and sucked at my pulse point, sending my need into overdrive.

When he unbuttoned my shirt, I knew my knees were too weak to stand after having gone so long without being touched, so I moved us over to the sofa.

He smiled at me and then slipped his shirt off. I couldn't help but stare. His body was so tight, so beautiful. I reached out and traced his washboard abs with my fingertips and glanced up as the heat in his eyes penetrated mine.

At that moment, things slowed. We were passionate, and I knew the sex would be intense, but I, well, I needed to feel everything. So I ran my hands down to his belt buckle without losing eye contact.

I let my fingers play along the edge of where his jeans met bared skin, and when he shuddered from my touch, I smiled. I missed having that kind of effect on a man. He watched me undo the beautiful belt buckle and unzip his jeans.

When I saw he wasn't wearing underwear, I almost lost the will to take it slow, but I forced myself to stay calm as his jeans slipped to the floor.

Manuel was uncut, and his cock stood at attention. I had resisted all I could. I pushed back his foreskin and let my tongue explore what became exposed. God he smelled so good, so masculine.

When I sucked his head into my mouth, he drew in a breath. *Screw slow*, I thought, and took his cock into my mouth until it hit the back of my throat.

"Fuck," he whispered, and I'd have chuckled if I hadn't had a mouth full of cock. I pulled back and sucked him deep into my throat again, then again, until I could feel him trembling. That's when I swallowed, and he called out my name. "Justin! Fuck, yeah!"

I pulled off and smiled up at him. His expression held so many feelings that I hesitated. This meant something to him. Of course it would.

"Sit down," I demanded. He did as I asked and plopped down on the sofa with his legs splayed wide. I knelt on the floor and finished taking my shirt off, then ran my hands up his muscular thighs and took his cock back into my mouth.

I was going to give this man so much pleasure it would cause him to explode. His moans and grunts only spurred me on. I loved sucking Manuel's beautiful thick, uncut cock, and I loved hearing him call my name in ecstasy.

I could tell he was about to come, and I was okay with that, but he gently pushed my head away, laughing. "No, mi amor, I want to see you have pleasure too," he said when I resisted. "Will you take your pants off for me? Let me see that pretty cock again?"

For a moment I didn't know what he meant. Then I remembered the day at the stream when he'd caught me skinny-dipping. I chuckled, then slowly let my pants drop. Like him, I wasn't wearing underwear. I seldom did. I preferred to let the boys swing free.

"Now, let me taste you," he said as he sat up and drew my body toward him. He didn't devour my cock like I had his. Instead, he lifted it to his mouth, looked at me from below, and slowly licked around my head.

When he sucked my cock into his mouth, he moaned around it, sending shivers up my body. He kept looking at me, watching as pleasure overtook me. Finally, he sucked me back into his throat, held me there for several moments, and then pulled back and did it again.

"God, you're... you're so good at this," I said and got a chuckle from him again.

He picked up speed while repeating the motion, sucking me deep and pulling back. I had to put my hands on his head to keep my balance. He smiled around the mouthful, and I could tell he wanted me to use him, so I did. I held his head in place and drove my cock into his mouth, thrusting my hips forward in a desperate rhythm.

His moans grew louder, and I was losing control. When he gripped my hips, stopping me, I thought maybe I'd done too much. But his hold turned into a caress, and he grinned up at me, then lay back against the cushions, inviting me to straddle him.

I didn't need to be asked twice. I scurried around the side of the sofa, arranged us in a sixty-nine position, and lined my cock up to his parted lips.

He grabbed my ass with both hands and shoved me inside his wet mouth, showing me he wanted it rough. I didn't hesitate and fucked deep into his throat with abandon. I took his cock in my mouth and held it there as I fucked him, his hands guiding me the whole time.

I wasn't even sucking him when his cock burst in my mouth, warm, tasty cum thick on my tongue.

"Mmm," I moaned as I lapped up all he had to give me. When he spasmed one last time, I leaned up and was about to move off of him, but his rough hands held me in place.

Without saying a word, he repositioned me so my ass was practically in his face. Then I felt the swipe of his tongue. "Oh God!" I cried out as he licked around my sensitive area. "Fuck, yeah, Manuel!"

I had only had that done to me once, while in college and before I started dating Donny. Not that he and I hadn't enjoyed a healthy sex life, but Donny just didn't find pleasure in rimming. I sure as hell was finding pleasure in it right now, though.

"God, Manuel," I choked out right before his probing tongue slid deep into my ass. I reached down to jack off, the pleasure too much to resist, but Manuel's hand slipped around mine and held it there. Fuck, I liked when he took control.

Maybe we both liked it, I thought before his tongue slipped out of my hole, sending me into a burst of ecstasy that caused all other thoughts to leave my head.

By the time he'd finished with my ass, I was a trembling ball of need. Desperate to be filled by his dick. I was usually a top, but fuck, all I could think of now was having more of Manuel inside me.

He gently nudged me, and I moved off him, then immediately lunged for his mouth to show him how much I enjoyed his talented tongue.

I felt the evidence first, then glanced down and saw his cock still standing to attention. I hadn't noticed when he was eating my ass. Nothing else registered while I was experiencing that much pleasure. Clearly, he'd found it pleasurable too.

"I, um, have a condom," Manuel said, sounding almost shy. "Can I fuck you?"

I cupped his face and kissed him again. "God, yes, I want that."

"Me too," he said and reached for his pants and pulled out a condom and a little tube of lube from a pocket.

"You came prepared?" I said, and he grinned sheepishly.

"A guy can hope, right?"

Manuel slipped the condom on, then pushed me back onto the sofa and lifted my legs to rest on his broad, tanned shoulders. He lubed my now loosened hole and his sheathed cock and then lined up to my entrance.

"Ready?" he whispered, and to show him just how ready I was, I attempted to thrust my ass onto his dick.

"Patience, mi amor, patience."

"Screw that, Manuel. Fuck me into this sofa!"

He chuckled but didn't make me wait any longer. His cock was thick, and as it entered me, it burned. But he was patient and allowed me to get used to him. Finally the burning subsided and I was able to allow him fully inside me.

It took a few moments of measured thrusts, but when I felt him flush against me, my nerves danced with pleasure. He kissed my neck tenderly and then unleashed his desire and pounded into me with abandon.

I reached up and grabbed the arm of the sofa to brace myself so I could take all this man had to give. Then I threw back my head, unable to form words amid the delightful onslaught.

"Goddamn, you feel good. So tight," he moaned as he thrust deeply into me in a steady rhythm.

I was beyond talking or even grunting. All I could think of was his big cock punishing my ass, owning it, giving me the kind of pleasure I never thought I'd have again.

My orgasm hit me strong. I blew so hard, I painted my chest and almost hit my eye.

Manuel pulled out, jerked off the condom, and stroked himself until he shot ribbons across my stomach and thighs.

Then he leaned over, licked at my cheek where some of my cum had landed, and gave me a taste in a heated kiss.

God help me, this man. What little was left of me melted right then and there.

He collapsed on top of me, and we both slipped in and out of consciousness, the intensity of our orgasms adding to the euphoria and afterglow.

Eventually, he crawled off me, glanced down at our cum-smeared bodies, and cocked an eyebrow in question. I pointed to the downstairs bathroom, where I'd stuffed a towel for when I came over to swim in the stream. I really did need to stock this place with some bare essentials, and soon.

Manuel returned with the towel and dried us both off, then climbed back onto the sofa and draped himself over me like a cozy blanket. That's how we fell asleep.

Maybe an hour passed before I began to wake. Manuel's delightful body heat warmed me, and his even breathing told me he was still asleep. It was wrong to think of Donny at that moment, but it was hard not to draw comparisons.

My boyfriend had been a great lover, attentive and satisfying, but the passion between us had never been as intense as what I felt with Manuel. Donny wasn't very creative in his lovemaking either, whereas I had a feeling Manuel had only just begun to show me his kinky side. That thought sent happy shivers through me. I wanted to explore with him.

More than anything, though, Manuel had given himself to me completely. He hadn't held back. He took pleasure in giving to his partner, and I loved that. I wanted to spend a lot more time with him, in and out of a bed.

Manuel

I USUALLY GOT up early on Saturdays to manage the cows and arrive at the butcher shop by ten to help out, since business had increased so much. Today… well, that wasn't the case.

I did feel a bit guilty about dropping the ball on the farm, but I knew I was a little obsessive about the cattle. They were fine, and tending to them couldn't compete with the nice, firm ass cuddled up against me this morning. Justin and I showered together as best as we could, considering we had no soap or shampoo, and our one towel was pretty used up from last night.

Regardless, we managed to get to the shop on time, and because they were already so busy when we got there, my nosy family couldn't harass us much. It had become a regular Saturday thing, serving a steady stream of customers right up to closing, since people wanted their barbecue for Sunday meals.

Justin danced around me as he got the chicken into the smoker. They'd figured out a routine of getting meats smoked and packaged the day before so people could pick them up early. María and Carlos started brisket and ribs in the mornings, at around ten, and Justin handled the meats that cooked faster. All in all, it meant we cooked barbecue all day long until we ran out.

Occasionally Justin dashed in with sides or other things he needed to bring up front. As usual, he didn't talk much while working, but today, unlike other Saturdays, he lingered and found subtle reasons to touch me. All without drawing the attention of my family, despite each point of contact sending electric pulses through my body.

Never in my life had I craved a man as much as I did Justin, and his gentle touches sent me into overdrive. By the time we closed up shop, I needed a cold shower or, better yet, another hot one shared with Justin. Unfortunately, since I'd neglected my morning farm chores, I had to make up for it that evening.

It turned out we had a near miss with the cows on Justin's land again, where the elk had yet again broken through another section of fence. Fortunately, I got it fixed before any cattle escaped. Still, it was getting dark before I returned home. I'd missed dinner, so I nuked the plate María left in the microwave for me and ate in the kitchen.

Part of me was relieved I'd missed the third degree that would've come my way had I been around that evening, even though on Saturday nights, the family usually kept to themselves because of the intensity of work. Even Antonio tended to go to his room early.

I texted Justin to tell him good night, and he replied almost instantly that he wished we'd had dinner together. I almost texted him back with a request to meet at his house, but then remembered that tomorrow would be an important day for all of us. Justin would be announcing his grocery store concept at our weekly family dinner.

Me: *We know neither one of us would get any rest if I came over tonight.*

Justin: *Valid point. I'll need all my wits about me for the big idea reveal.*

Me: *Maybe we could spend tomorrow night together? I know where I can get a bed for your house.*

Justin: *Yes, please, after we finish with Sunday dinner.*

Me: *If we survive it.*

He sent back a laughing emoji, and I put my phone down and closed my eyes. I was falling for Justin so hard, but I'd known that I would. I just hoped I wasn't moving too fast. It was one thing to share a great night of sex, but another thing altogether to be thinking of sharing a life with him.

He'd told me to take it slow, and I was trying, but my heart burned hot. In retrospect, I probably shouldn't have agreed to that because I didn't think I was capable of going slow with Justin. That didn't mean I couldn't give him time to find his footing. I'd give him every opportunity to pump the brakes, but he had to be the driver on that.

Like last night when we'd waltzed together for the first time, I couldn't deny feeling like we were meant for each other. We just fit together a little too perfectly, physically and in all the other ways that mattered.

I woke up early and dashed out to complete my long list of farm chores so I had time to shower before Justin came over. He liked to help María prepare the food, so he usually arrived for Sunday dinners around lunchtime.

Papá had told me to call him so he and Mamá could hear the family conversation about the grocery store. I agreed, but only if they didn't tell anyone in advance they would be listening. If my brothers knew Papá was on the line, it might prevent them from being brutally honest. I also didn't want the family to be influenced by the possibility of Mamá and Papá coming to live here.

Too much was at stake with Justin investing his life savings, along with the financial risks we would be taking, for anyone to hold back from saying their piece. This needed to be a financial and business decision first and a family decision second. My parents agreed on the need to be discreet, so I figured out a plan to slip out of the room to call them, then come back and set my phone on the table so they could hear everything.

I didn't pretend not to be excited when Justin showed up. I had just finished my shower, and I came downstairs as he walked into the house. I made a beeline for him and kissed his handsome face. "I missed you," I whispered, and I enjoyed seeing those adorable cheeks blush.

"Good to see you two are getting along," Cassie said as she closed the front door.

I winked at her and then took Justin's hand and led him into the kitchen. "Oh, Justin, you're just in time," María said. "Can you make—"

My sister-in-law took over and shooed me out of the room. Having been effectively dismissed, I went to the living room and joined my brothers in front of the TV for an English Football League game.

I dozed off, only to wake up to Carlos and Martín teasing about the old man sleeping while watching the game. I flipped them off just as María came in and told us to set the table. It was a Sunday ritual that we all did on autopilot.

When my brothers and Antonio took their seats at the table, I went into the kitchen to help bring out the food. So many people in such a small space required us to be organized. Justin had taken on the serving responsibilities these past few months, but I still liked to contribute.

He kissed me and then handed me a bowl to take to the dining room. María cocked an eyebrow but didn't say anything, but I knew she wouldn't remain silent for long. My sister-in-law wasn't known for keeping quiet about anything to do with love and romance.

We sat around the big dining room table, Justin seated beside me like usual. Carlos said the blessing like he always did, and Antonio again had to be reminded that he wasn't the only person eating a meal.

Justin seemed to enjoy messing with Antonio more than the rest of us, and since he sat between Antonio and me, it was often Justin slapping my nephew's hand away to give the rest of us a chance at each dish. He also didn't hold back in ribbing the boy over stuff, giving as good as he got. It warmed my heart to see my guy so close to my family.

Carlos and Martín were in charge of cleaning up, something Cassie demanded shortly after moving in. "Men can't just sit around while women do all the work," she'd said. My brothers adored her, so no arguments were ever made.

Secretly, I was proud of my family for stepping up to do the right thing despite customs that dictated otherwise. I wondered if that would remain when Mamá and Papá moved here.

That reminded me I needed to call them before we all reassembled around the table for dessert and our weekly business meeting. So I disappeared into the bathroom and made my call. "Hola, Papá," I said and confirmed we were about to begin the conversation. "Remember, don't let them know you're listening until they agree to Justin's plan."

"Of course, hijo," he said.

"Is Mamá there too?" I asked.

"Sí, hijo," she said. "I'm excited for you. I can't wait to meet this Justin."

I smiled, knowing my mamá would love him as much as the rest of my family did.

"Okay, I'm going back so they don't get suspicious," I said, slipping out of the bathroom and returning to the dining table.

I set my phone next to my dessert plate, and no one paid it any mind. Justin had been practicing making flan, and as much as I liked my guy, I didn't like his latest creation. He'd gotten in the habit of testing out desserts with us on Sundays to get our opinions. Today, at least, the flan wasn't just a bowl of sweet scrambled eggs. He was getting better, but it still wasn't quite ready for human consumption.

"So, I have a business proposal," Justin began. "I want you to hear me out before you say no."

Everyone's eyes turned toward him, and I touched his leg in support. "I... well, I think I might have found a place for us to expand."

He spent the next half hour talking about the grocery store in impressive detail. The more information Justin shared, the more it became clear why I wasn't in charge of the day-to-day management of our butcher shop. For instance, I hadn't considered the cost difference between what we paid in leasing the Northport shop and the projected mortgage payment for the Wilcox grocery store. All told, the switch would have us paying slightly less each month but for considerably more space.

"Here's a diagram of the store," Justin said, passing a printout around the table. "As you can see, there's an old sandwich shop on the side of the grocery where we could put the butcher shop. It's the same size as the shop in Northport, and it could have its own entrance."

I watched as my family took in what Justin was saying. My brothers were smiling, which was a good sign. María was not, which was a bad sign. None of my family members hid their feelings well.

"You aren't afraid we'll lose business if we move out of Northport?" Cassie looked at María as if she wanted her to answer.

Justin nodded. "I suspect we will lose some of our customer base, at least initially, but consider my projections. Before the grocery store closed, it made significantly more than I think we'd lose if we moved. Wilcox is still on the interstate, so there's no reason why our out-of-town customer traffic should slow down. In fact, being closer to Eugene should help us. Locally, I think lots of Northport customers would readily travel to Wilcox to buy from us. After all, we and any number of folks commute between the two towns daily and don't think much of it."

María and Cassie quizzed Justin while my brothers and I just listened. I glanced over several times at Carlos, who wasn't known for being quiet regarding business matters. The smile had not left his face since the conversation started.

That was strange, but I figured the best thing I could do was let things unfold without interfering. Justin was doing a great job without my help, and he fielded the onslaught of questions from my sisters-in-law like a pro. With so many numbers being thrown around by the three of them, and only occasionally Carlos, my head felt like it was going to explode.

Finally, María pushed back from the table, a smile spreading across her face. "It's a good idea, and one Carlos and I were talking about ourselves," she said. "Wilcox is growing. We've seen it since they began restoring the covered bridges. We've wanted to get involved and talked about setting up a satellite store. Dios dirá."

"God willing," I explained when Justin looked to me, confused.

His smile brightened. "So, two places," Martín said, breaking his silence. "How will we staff both? I mean, we barely keep things going as it is."

"¡Hijos!" Papá exclaimed, shocking everyone.

I laughed and pointed at my phone on the table as María looked me in the eye. "We will open the new butcher shop for you," Papá said, "provided you think your old padres can do so."

I had to interpret what they said to Justin, who chuckled quietly. No one was going to say no to our parents, especially when our papá challenged them with his age.

"Papá, you're willing to move here? What about your house?" Carlos asked.

"Sí, mijo, your mother misses you. The house is a building, family is home."

I smiled at how true the sentiment was and at our papá's amusing way of admitting he missed us too. But we tried to never dwell on how far apart we lived, since that only brought sadness. "Papá, when can you come?"

"Soon. Will you have a place for us to stay? Is the house big enough?"

María cringed before she could stop herself, and when Justin looked confused, I whispered what he'd asked. Then a determined expression crossed his face.

"Señor López, this is Justin Latham. It's a pleasure to meet you, sir. I have a home nearby that's sitting empty. I'm happy to let you and Señora López stay there while we set things up."

My mouth fell open at the offer. "Justin, it's too much," I said, and he raised his hand.

"No, Manuel, I need your parents' help as much as you do. This is my business as well, remember? I can stay with my uncles as long as necessary, and your mamá and papá can stay at the farmhouse."

"No, not necessary," Mamá said. "If you let us stay, we would welcome you to be with us. Besides, I hear wonderful things about you."

Her saying that made the backs of my eyes sting, but I forced down the emotion so as not to embarrass myself.

Justin smiled. "I'd like that very much, ma'am," he said.

The rest of the conversation was about moving my parents up to Oregon. The tourism market had grown significantly since we left El Paso, so Mamá had already found someone to rent their house once the weather turned cooler.

It surprised me how much they'd planned since I called them a few days earlier. "Mamá," I said when I remembered Justin saying he wanted to visit El Paso someday, "I can come pick you up, and maybe Justin will come with me. We'll bring the truck and our big trailer to move your stuff. Besides, I want to show Justin the festival, which is next month, right?"

"Sí, hijo, it is. Yes, that's perfect." I heard Mamá ask Papá if they could be packed by then, and he quickly said they could. Their home was small. Our family had barely fit in it once my brothers and I hit our teens. Mamá had kept it beautiful with little Talavera pots filled with flowers. It was no surprise they could use it as a vacation rental.

When everyone had talked the situation to death, we hung up and I walked Justin outside so I could speak to him privately about his offer.

"You know you don't have to."

"Stop, Manuel. I'd already decided to offer when you told me they were considering moving here. I don't need all that house. In fact, as much as I love the renovations, I was dreading moving into it by myself."

He paused and gazed out over the pastures and then looked back at me. "Manuel, the house is so different now from when I grew up there. Walls have been moved and modern appliances have been added to the kitchen, but it's still the same house at the end of the day. Sometimes, when I'm there alone, the bad memories are too strong to forget. I-I was worried I wouldn't be able to live there. You have to understand with your parents moving in, we are rewriting the story about that home for me. We're filling it with love, family, and hope. The future is so much brighter than my past. Can you see that?"

For a moment, the desperation on Justin's face gave me pause. But I understood. "Sí, amor, I do now."

A tear fell from his eye before he buried his face in my shoulder. "Thank you, Manuel. I really do need this."

I shook my head as I pulled Justin into an embrace. My heart was overflowing so much it was hard to say anything without getting emotional. I knew deep down in my soul, Mamá and Papá were the perfect people to help heal Justin's heart and create him new, happier memories at the farmstead.

I could already see Mamá out back hanging up her clothes, something she still did even in the dusty El Paso summers, saying they smelled better than when dried inside. I bet Papá would take an interest in the covered bridges around Wilcox, including the one near Justin's farm. Hell, he might even be up for a plunge in the swimming hole over there. Yeah, my family would make Justin's house feel like a home again. I had no doubt.

Justin

KNOWING I HAD to furnish the farmhouse and not knowing how long the Lópezes would be staying, I had asked Manuel to set up communication between his parents and me. It only took a few days before Señora López got my phone number and bypassed Manuel altogether.

I could tell he wasn't exactly happy about that. Still, after having such a horrible relationship with Donny's family, I took advantage of starting off on such a good note with his parents. Señora López and I spoke almost daily and had for the past month.

I'd told Manuel I wanted to go slow, but damn, that definitely wasn't his family's default speed. Apparently, my heart wasn't that interested in taking things slow with Manuel either. I missed him when he wasn't close by, let alone wrapped in my arms, but we didn't get to spend the night together often, even after he found the perfect bed for my bedroom.

Cassie and María took me to an estate sale near Wilcox where I found several pieces of old brown furniture. I didn't love the color, but María convinced me that Manuel's mother would want to paint everything anyway. As evidence she showed me pictures of Manuel's childhood home, which was awash in bright colors.

I was chomping at the bit, as my grandmother used to say, for the Lópezes to get here so we could bring life to the house. And they were bringing quite a few pieces of furniture with them. "I don't want tourists to destroy our heirlooms," Señora López told me when she texted a picture of an amazing but enormous buffet that'd be making the move.

I measured the dining space to confirm the piece would fit perfectly, and I was already imagining what the combination of their precious furniture and my secondhand pieces would look like throughout the house.

María and Cassie convinced the brothers to hire help for the butcher shop. "With Justin and Manuel off to El Paso, we need extra hands to prepare the meat and cook the sides," María argued.

Carlos wasn't convinced, but now that I knew what was required to manage the shop, there was no way their parents could run the shop alone in Wilcox. In fact, since the cat had gotten out of the bag thanks to my uncles, interest in the Wilcox store had caused the number of customers coming to Northport to double. "We can't wait until you open. Oh, it's such a relief, knowing we'll have a grocery in town again," Mayor Polly said when she and her husband, Tim, came to check out the shop in Northport.

I hated to tell Carlos, but we'd be hiring a lot more people if our new venture took off like we thought it might.

Manuel and I took our time on the drive down to El Paso. "This will be the end of our privacy," he told me the night before we left. His strong arms wrapped tightly around me, and I lost myself in the feel of his bigger body. God, I loved being held by him.

"I don't know. I have a plan up my sleeve about that," I admitted. I didn't go into detail, but the grocery store had a second floor where the main office used to be. It was just under a thousand square feet, which wasn't huge, but adequate for what I had in mind. It also had an exterior exit and a full bathroom, including a shower. At one time there had been a little kitchenette up there too, but someone had removed the appliances long ago and left only the old plywood cabinets.

The place was clad in ugly wood paneling from the nineteen sixties, but I'd already fixed that by painting the walls. I also pulled the carpet out and discarded it with crap from the old sandwich shop that'd been stored up there. We could—and probably should—fix it up as an apartment to rent out, but selfishly, I wanted it to be our little love nest.

I was beyond excited to have Manuel's parents living in my childhood home. That was a blessing in every way, but there was no way in hell I would give up needed private time with my man—not now I'd gotten a taste of him.

The fact that none of Manuel's family had discovered the little office made me that much happier. Sure, they'd eventually figure things out, especially since a staircase led from the storage area into the loft, but for now it was a delightful little secret. I couldn't wait to share it with Manuel when we returned from El Paso.

From the moment we set foot into Casa López, I felt like I'd been embraced in a giant hug. The home was bright, inviting, and had a lot of personality, just as I'd envisioned. I already knew his parents liked me and accepted my relationship with their son, and that went a long way to ease my anxiety at meeting them in person.

"Justin, oh, you are even more handsome in person," Manuel's mamá said as she hugged me. Of course, when Señor López grabbed my hand and shook it tightly, then said the same thing Manuel had said he would on our first date, I had to stifle my grin.

"We're both happy to meet you, son," Señor López said. And I could tell they meant it.

During the day, we helped load boxes onto the trailer. Then all four of us went to the festival in the evenings. "You can dance like that?" I asked when I remembered Manuel had told me he used to perform.

"Oh, he was the best," Señor López proudly said.

The folkloric dances were truly amazing, with the perfect timing between the male and female dancers. It was as if you could get lost in the movement, almost as if you were being transported into some magical fairyland. Suddenly I wanted him to teach me how to do the women's part. Even though I'd said I would, I had no interest in dressing in Mexican drag, although the skirts were genuinely impressive. I simply wanted to learn to dance like that with my man wearing the embroidered and black *traje de charro* we saw the male dancers wearing. *My boyfriend.* But it was too soon to call him that.

When we loaded the last of the boxes on our final day there, I could tell the Lópezes were struggling with leaving. Manuel came around the trailer as his parents stood in the doorway, staring into their little house. "Go, be with them," I said. "I'm going to take a walk before we leave."

He kissed me and then went to stand between his parents. I lingered momentarily, and my heart filled as I watched Manuel put his arms around them. Then I walked in the opposite direction.

I had never had a home mean so much to me that I would struggle to leave it. My own house was anything but a good place for me, but hopefully that was about to change. I thought good things about my uncle's home. I'd only really been a guest there—an extended-stay guest at various points in my life—but I'd never considered it *my* home.

The house I lived in with Donny was sweet, but I always knew his parents resented me being there. That tainted it for me, and as much as I loved nesting there, I didn't miss it when I left.

This house, however, meant a lot to Manuel's entire family. He and his brothers had grown up there, and every nook and cranny was filled with memories. Of course it was difficult for them to leave it. I almost felt bad that they were having to, but they'd rarely make new family memories by staying. All three of their sons, their two daughters-in-law, and their only grandchild, were in Oregon and most likely would be for years to come.

With how family-oriented these folks were, I knew relocating was the right choice for them, even if it was a painful one.

By the time I circled the neighborhood, Señora López was in the truck's back seat and Manuel was in the driver's seat. I didn't hesitate to scoot into the back with Manuel's mamá, allowing his father to sit up front. Manuel looked shocked when I crawled into the back, but there was plenty of driving ahead for us to switch.

For now, I wanted nothing more than to get to know my new roommates. If our phone conversations were any indication of how things would go, we were going to have an enjoyable drive back to Oregon.

Manuel

JUSTIN'S LAUGH filled the pickup as Mamá showed him pictures of me when I was little. She'd brought two old family albums with her instead of packing them into the back. I groaned when she told him stories of the shenanigans Martín and I got into when we were kids.

Carlos was so much older that he seldom got into trouble with us, although more than a few times, he got into trouble *because* of us. Justin truly enjoyed the stories, especially the embarrassing ones. He sounded delighted and carefree when he laughed, and the sound filled my heart so much I couldn't help but smile.

We stopped in New Mexico to refill the tank and for Mamá to stretch her legs. As I pumped gas, Papá got out and stood with me. "This one has stolen your heart," he said, more as a statement than question.

I smiled but didn't respond. It's not like I could deny it. "Carlos said he lost someone. That he was broken when he came to be with you all."

I nodded, and my smile disappeared. "Sí, Papá, he had a tough time. It took a lot of work for him to let me in."

"But does he know you are in love with him?" Papá asked. I'm not sure why it surprised me he should ask. My parents never hesitated to inquire about anything in our lives, no matter how uncomfortable or sensitive the conversation.

"It's too soon for me to declare my love for him, Papá. He's still vulnerable."

"No, hijo, it's never too soon to tell someone you care about that you have feelings for them. A man like that is special. He will need to know how you feel soon, especially when he is stuck living with us."

I chuckled. "His idea, Papá, not mine. He said he wants you and Mamá to help fill his old home with good memories instead of the old painful ones. His father… hurt him," I said, not wanting to go into detail. If Justin wanted to share his past with my parents, that'd be his choice.

Papá sighed. "My father was difficult. He had too many children, too many responsibilities, and a love for tequila. I know something of the need to replace bad memories with good. You know your mamá and I will love him, if only because you do. I'm guessing we'll come to love him ourselves because he has a good heart."

I smiled and quickly put the gas hose back up to distract myself from becoming emotional. Not that Papá had ever cared if my brothers or I cried. He was a man of strong emotions and never hesitated to express them. But I didn't want Justin to see me being too gushy, certainly not while standing at a random gas pump with my father. Thinking Justin viewed me as some stoic cowboy type was probably delusional at this point, but he had yet to learn I was a big marshmallow inside.

Mamá and Justin returned to the truck carrying bags of food we'd never finish if we had double the miles to get back to Oregon. But I could tell they were bonding, which my family tended to do over food—even gas station fare, apparently.

The trip was long, but we stayed in good spirits. We spent a night in Medford instead of driving through, which meant we arrived in Wilcox early the next day. Knowing the family couldn't greet us, since they were all working at the shop, made me a little sad. But that's the reality of a busy family.

Justin and I helped unload everything from the trailer. Mamá directed where she wanted the furniture placed, though Justin seemed to already know. I hadn't been included in their phone conversations for a while, but apparently they'd planned everything.

Once they were unpacked, I looked around and felt my heart swell. Justin's house was nothing like what we'd left in El Paso, but decorated with Mamá's furniture, it felt very much like home. She also had grand plans to paint and beautify the ugly brown pieces Justin, María, and Cassie had found at an estate sale. I gave Mamá one week, two max, before she made the home as welcoming as our beloved childhood one.

The fact that Justin seemed to be nestling into the transformation gave me hope and pause. Would this be too much? Would he end up retreating to his uncles'? I didn't know how to process it all. That didn't mean I wasn't happy. Maybe I was happier than I'd ever been, but I was concerned about him.

Once my parents settled in, I excused myself to check on the cattle. Way too many days had gone by with the farm in the hands of my not-so-capable brothers. Carlos was a financial genius. Martín was good with his hands, which is why he was our head butcher. But neither of them nor my charismatic nephew were known for doing much farm work.

Justin returned to his uncles' place, saying he needed to check on them. I knew he wanted to give my parents some private time to adjust. Fortunately, the farm didn't appear any worse for wear. I would have to begin haying this week, but thankfully, we'd had rains this summer. So, unlike the spring haying season, the pastures were lush once again.

Surprising because of how much inventory we were selling, we still had a small surplus of steers, which was good. We'd have to be able to feed them, though. Hay was still expensive, so I preferred to store as much as possible. There was no rest for the weary, so I'd be on the tractor first thing tomorrow morning.

I ended up going home and crawling into bed. I hadn't gotten much sleep the past few days, mostly because I was so anxious about getting home, so I fell asleep immediately, thinking about the trip.

Life was really good right now. Papá hadn't been wrong. I needed to tell Justin how I felt, and I would do that as soon as we had time to ourselves again.

IT TOOK an entire month of long days and sleepless nights to set up the butcher shop in Wilcox. With the exhausting summer heat, by the time we finally got the health department out to inspect and give the go-ahead, none of us had the energy to open the place. "Why don't we plan for a grand opening in a couple of weeks," Justin offered when we all met at his house that Sunday for dinner.

We still usually had our family meals at home, even though Justin's house was much more open and the dining table more accommodating for our large family. However, some strange dynamics were going on between María and Mamá.

I'd mentioned it, only for Papá to tell me to keep my mouth shut. "Women need to establish boundaries. Don't interfere," he said, and the strained look on Carlos's face made me want to laugh out loud. Cassie and Justin were involved in all the dynamics too, but unlike the other two women in our lives, Cassie was the queen of laid-back.

She and Martín were almost the same in that regard. Every time I saw Justin, he was smiling at something Mamá or the sisters-in-law had said. He was in his element, all working together to prepare food for the shop.

Shifting dynamics aside, having the parents around had taken stress off all of us—especially me. Papá split his time between the shop and the farm, helping manage the cattle while I did the haying. They also helped us finally begin to meet customer demand for smoked meat and sides, not to mention all the meat we prepped in the butcher shop. I almost regretted that we'd be splitting the party between two locations.

After everyone agreed with Justin's idea to slightly delay the Wilcox store opening so we could rest up, María cleared her throat. "I have another idea." She bit her bottom lip, and our usually strong-spirited María seemed unsure of herself.

She looked at Carlos, who nodded slightly. Then she glanced at Justin and sighed. "I know this will be difficult to hear, especially for you, Justin, who's invested so much money, but I… we have struggled finding people to work for us in Northport, and the landlord has told us he is raising the rent in January. Not by a lot, but if we sign a lease, it'll mean we're stuck there for another three years."

She swallowed hard, and Carlos reached over and took her hand. "I think we should close the shop in Northport. I-I think we should put all our efforts into getting the shop and the grocery store set up in Wilcox before the holiday season arrives."

Justin cocked his head as if it was a surprise. Had María really not talked to him about it? From his reaction, I had to think maybe not. I watched the entire family as we took in María's suggestion.

I can't say I was shocked. We knew we would eventually go in that direction, even if it was risky, but I trusted Justin and his uncles' projections. "I'm in favor," I said, drawing the attention off María and onto me. My sister-in-law gave me a grateful look.

"Listen, I'm exhausted. It's been a horrible year with the drought and surplus of cattle, not to mention the two years of drought we had before. Moving over to Wilcox will save us having to buy another expensive smoker, and I can easily resell all the secondhand equipment we already bought for the place. Let's continue building buzz for the relocation and get the grocery side up to speed, then close up shop for a couple of weeks in August and move."

The room erupted, and Justin listened attentively to it all, although I did wonder how much of the Spanish he caught. He understood more than he used to, but the conversations were very quick.

Finally Carlos put his hand up. "Familia, for something like this," he said, "we need to vote. Are we ready to do that now?"

Everyone, including Justin, nodded. I'd already said my piece. "Okay, raise your hand if you think we should close the Northport shop and relocate to Wilcox."

I smiled as every hand, including Antonio's, rose. "Well, I think it's decided, then. We are moving to Wilcox."

Beneath everyone's excitement, I could tell there was just as much reluctance. We had unanimously voted to do something very scary and risky. However, I knew we were all tapped out. There were just so many hours in the day. Two shops would be too much to handle. Relocating was the right choice, even if we made less money.

When I glanced at Justin, he made eye contact and smiled. I knew he wanted time alone with me to chat. Since my brothers had cleanup duty, which Papá had taken to as well, no one would miss us if we slipped out for a bit.

I stood and drew Justin up with me. "Why don't we take a drive," I suggested as we left the house.

He nodded. "Yeah, I've got something I wanted to show you anyway. Wanna drive, or do you want me to?"

"I'll drive. Where are we headed?" I asked.

"The grocery store in Wilcox."

I groaned and Justin snickered. Obviously, he'd known I hoped we were going somewhere to celebrate the new decision by getting naked. Oh well, that was what it meant to be in business with the man you loved. Work was as much a part of our lives as anything else.

"Whatever you want," I said, and we climbed into my truck and drove into town.

Justin

THINGS HAD been so busy since we returned from El Paso that I hadn't had time to show Manuel my love-nest project.

There were several pieces of furniture Señora López hadn't wanted, and not willing to toss them, I'd brought them to the love nest.

I spent several nights—time I was supposed to be at my uncles'—painting and decorating, and the result was a vibrant yet relaxing aesthetic.

I found a nice headboard and reasonably priced mattress online and effectively converted the back office into a bedroom. The living room and kitchenette had windows that looked down into the store itself, and even with heavy curtains, it made me uncomfortable thinking our intimate moments could be exposed for all to see. So the small, windowless back office was the best choice for our bed.

When I told Uncle Henry what I was up to, he and Uncle Jeff came over, checked the place out, and recommended where to get slightly used kitchen cabinets we could install cheaply. That was good, considering that between the farmhouse remodel and the store venture, my savings were pretty much tapped out. I painted the cabinets a soft yellow, and I also installed and painted Talavera-like tiles—a decorative touch I hoped Manuel would appreciate.

With my mini remodel complete, the apartment looked cute. The hodgepodge of stuff added to its charm. Most importantly, it was comfortable enough for what I had in mind, and so having it completed as much as I ever would, I decided to tell Manuel.

I had no idea María was going to spring such a monumental surprise on us tonight regarding closing down the Northport shop, but I had seen the landlord show up twice. On the first visit he said the neighboring businesses were complaining about our queues, and I guessed that the second time was when he actually informed María he'd be raising the rent.

I wondered if the landlord could've foreseen his actions would lead to him losing one of his strongest anchors. The man was arrogant and unfriendly, and I liked the idea of our monthly rent money going toward the grocery store mortgage—which I'd been paying—instead of into that man's pocket.

I never minded investing in the López family business, which was clearly paying off. Carlos had spent a lot of time reviewing the finances with Uncle Jeff and me, ensuring we had a fair cut of the profits, which was becoming significant. The whole thing had been a great business decision, not to mention the fact that I had gained some wonderful friends.

We parked in front of the grocery store, and I almost asked Manuel to pull around back, but his pouty look caused me to chuckle inside. He clearly thought we were here to work, so I decided to keep up the pretense.

Since the townsfolk tended to wander inside out of curiosity when the doors weren't locked, I locked the front door behind us and grabbed Manuel's hand. I led him through the maze of stuff from the previous occupants that we wanted to save but didn't have any use for yet.

When we reached the storage area, I stopped and turned toward him. "Have you ever wondered what's up there?" I asked, pointing at the staircase.

Manuel looked confused, then shrugged. "I just assumed it was more storage. Why? Do we have a leak coming from there or something?"

I bit the inside of my cheek to keep up the charade. "Come on, let's go check it out," I said, leading the way up the stairs.

Only a couple of windows faced outside, so it was pretty dark even after I opened the door. When Manuel stepped inside, I flipped the lights on and watched him take in the space.

"What?" he asked, turning in circles. "What is this? An apartment?"

"Yes," I said, "sorta."

"To rent?" he asked, confused.

"Well, we probably should to save money, but…." I said as I took his hand and led him to the rear of the apartment. "I thought we might find a better use for the place."

Manuel's eyes grew large when he saw the bed. Then a mischievous smile crossed his lips and he turned toward me. "This is for us?" he asked, almost whispering, and I laughed out loud.

"Yes, just for us—our private little quarters until your family figures out it's here. Not that I plan on giving them the key."

"We should tear out the stairs, safer bet," he said as he pushed me toward the bed.

I laughed as I fell onto my back and Manuel pounced, wasting no time unbuttoning my shirt.

We weren't able to get away to have sex often. It'd been over a week since we'd met in my bedroom while his family worked. I could tell Manuel felt guilty over stealing time together, but it was stolen moments like that during the day or nothing at all.

"When did you do all this?" Manuel asked a while later as he lay half across my very satiated body.

"In the evenings. My uncles helped."

"Ugh, that means they know this is here."

I chuckled. "They do, but I don't think they'll be blabbing about our little love nest."

He leaned up on his elbow and looked down at me. "I've missed having you to myself."

"Don't get me wrong, I love your family, and having your mom and dad at the house has done wonders. But I need *you* time. When you and I can just do this, you know?" I asked.

He nodded. "Same, but I haven't known how to make that happen."

I reached up and ran my fingers through the silky threads of his hair. "When I discovered this, I knew it could be our own private place. I-I thought we'd have more time before we opened the grocery store, but now—"

"But now, we're moving forward quicker."

"Exactly. So we better enjoy this while it lasts," I said, which got a chuckle out of him.

"Oh, mi guapo, I plan to."

Manuel

THREE DAYS. That's all it took for my nosy sister-in-law to discover the upstairs office was a love shack.

Justin and I had accidentally left the door unlocked when we came down on Sunday, and a few days later, María and Carlos spent a morning there checking out the store to devise a plan for next steps. In exploring the space, María walked up and into the apartment. I'd left my hat on the little red dining table, set for two, and she figured it out immediately. Late that afternoon I arrived at the Northport shop to deliver the last of the meat from the home freezers, and María laughed upon seeing me. She pulled Justin and me out into the back and told us she'd found our secret.

Justin blushed, and I just shook my head. "You're like a little terrier," I said, getting another laugh. "Can you keep it a secret for now? Mamá and Papá are in Justin's house. Our home is too busy, and Justin isn't comfortable going to his uncles' place for us to have alone time."

"My lips are sealed, but you know it won't stay a secret if you leave the door unlocked," she'd said, and she chuckled as she walked back into the shop to finish closing up.

"Well, crap," Justin said.

"It's okay. She won't tell. I was only ten when she and Carlos were dating and got married, but I remember they were always looking for alone time. If anyone gets it, she does."

Justin smiled and leaned into me. "I don't mind if they know, but I'd rather we tell everyone than have it be gossipy. In fact, I think maybe we should move there. I'm not saying we move in together officially, but you know, it wouldn't hurt to stay there when we're working long hours, right?"

I was shocked. Granted, I liked the idea a lot, but I was also afraid. It wasn't long ago Justin was pumping the brakes on even starting a relationship. Was he pushing for this? "Justin, I think it's too fast for that." I put my hand over his heart. "You were hurt so badly, and I promised to go slow. That's the opposite of slow."

He sighed but nodded. "You're right. I guess I was getting ahead of myself, but things are happening so fast."

"They are, and we'll roll with the punches, but right now, we'll use your secret apartment for us time. When it's time for more, we'll both know. There's no need to rush into anything you'll regret."

"Me? What about you?" he asked.

I just smiled. "Justin, my heart is full of you. It sings beautiful ballads when you're in my presence. I don't think you can drive me away now, but I want to honor the love you had and lost. I'm willing to give you all the space you need to heal, okay?"

He leaned over and kissed me, and then Antonio walked out and made gagging noises. "Dude, you're such a buzzkill," Justin said. "Come over here and help me wash out the inside of the smoker. Water only. Don't you dare use soap."

I smiled as Justin oversaw my impulsive nephew through all the work of putting the smokers to sleep, as he called it.

I left after that to get back to the farm. The breeding process had begun, and our bull was enormous. I wanted to ensure he didn't get too amorous with the cows and accidentally hurt them.

Over the next few weeks, I knew we'd be intensely busy. On Sunday, Justin's uncle Henry asked to join us at our weekly family dinner to discuss something. Not even Justin knew what he wanted.

Our house was too small to accommodate everyone who ate with us now, so we met at Justin's home. Mamá, Justin, and María had taken over the kitchen, kicking poor Cassie out. Not that she minded. She'd been feeling poorly lately.

The dining table Justin and my sisters-in-law had hauled back from an estate sale was ugly as homemade sin, but big enough to easily accommodate all of us, although we had to bring chairs from home. Mamá had already decided she was going to paint it in "more spirited colors," and I was secretly looking forward to that.

Mamá was traditional in her style choices. "I grew up when people weren't afraid of color," she liked to say. She wasn't wrong about changing styles. Even before we moved up to Oregon, the stores in Juarez had begun to stock more neutral furniture. I was pleased Mamá wasn't afraid of the bright colors of our Mexican heritage.

When Henry and Jeff showed up for dinner, the family pulled them into our crazy lives. We ate too much, thanks to Mamá's input, and after a quick cleanup, we reassembled to discuss business.

Henry stood up. "So, I understand this is when you all discuss and make decisions, and I have news about the grocery store." The exchange of furtive glances around the table was almost comical. Everyone appeared curious. "We promised Justin we would look into having a fundraiser or the like to help set up the grocery store, and I think we might have found a way."

He had our attention now. "Um, Jeffrey, this was your doing. Do you want to explain?" Henry asked.

Jeff nodded and stood. "I've spoken to the mayor. She and the county commissioner have petitioned an Oregon-based foundation whose mission is to help support food safety networks in small towns like Wilcox. They would like to meet you all tomorrow, if possible, to go over the grant details."

As was our way, we peppered Justin's uncles with questions, but Jeff kept saying we needed to speak to the mayor.

"Thank you all again for dinner," Henry announced when the conversation died down. "Jeff and I should take our leave and give you the space you need to discuss this matter further."

"Oh no," Papá said. "Today isn't the day to do that. You are our guests, and we still have dessert. I understand Justin has been perfecting his hand at *un postre de Mexico*."

Justin smiled and jumped up. "I have. In fact, I've made *pastel de hojaldre*. Did I say that correctly?"

"Muy bien," Mamá said, probably to keep Antonio from telling Justin he'd mispronounced *pastel*. When she gave her grandson the stink eye, I knew that's precisely why she intervened.

"Señora López has been helping me learn to make this, thinking it would be good to sell at the store. It's hard to make, though. I might not have done it correctly."

I got up and helped him serve the cake, and then we all dug in. It wasn't Mamá's by any means. It was a little dry, but it wasn't bad for his first try. Not even Antonio complained. Okay, he wasn't likely to complain about much involving food. My nephew had just hit another growth spurt, making him taller than anyone in our family. Papá said it was because of our Cocopá roots. He'd always said we were descended from the legendary giant Native tribe of Arizona. I figured the kid kept growing because he wouldn't stop eating.

As the family sat around talking, asking Henry and Jeff about local stuff since they'd both lived in Wilcox longer than any of us, I realized this marked the first time our entire family had gathered together. Obviously, Mamá and Papá were here now, but all the in-laws as well. Both my sisters-in-law had been folded into our family nearly from the day they started dating my brothers, though their parents had not.

María's parents, who were older when she was born, passed away many years ago. Cassie had grown up in foster care, and although she had foster parents, she didn't consider them her family. That was reserved for us. But Justin brought with him Henry and Jeff, who were more like fathers than uncles and who I already considered my in-laws.

My heart swelled, and when Justin looked at me, his smile matched mine. We were all close, sitting around the table. When he leaned over and snuggled into my side, I couldn't remember a time that I'd ever been this happy.

The next day, María, Carlos, Justin, and I gathered at the mayor's office in Wilcox while the rest of the family kept the shop going in Northport.

Both Mayor Polly and Ellen McLeroy, the county commissioner, were there.

"It's my understanding that Jeff has filled you in on some of the details," Mayor Polly said, "but we want to go over the finer points because you must understand what the grant will and won't pay for."

Between Mayor Polly and Mrs. McLeroy, they filled us in on the particulars. "You can hire staff for the grocery store, and the city will distribute funds for their pay. Of course, our first goal is to provide jobs for those who lost them when Bellingham's went out of business."

We were all shocked—in a good way—when they told us the dollar amount. "Do we have to pay it back?" I asked.

"No," the commissioner said. "This is a full grant the city will manage on your behalf."

"So, are Bellingham's former employees still around?" I asked.

The mayor shrugged. "Yes, mostly. Some have retired or moved on, but the store hasn't been closed too terribly long. I think you'll find many who worked here would like to return, given the chance. We'd provide a list of those folks."

"So, other than the rehires, what do we need to do for the grant?" María asked.

"Well, Henry and Tim, my husband, have already begun setting up all the legal documents you'll have to sign. Then we have to get the city council to agree to the plan, which won't be a problem, I can assure you," the mayor said.

It all sounded so good, maybe too good to be true.

"Can we get back to you?" María asked, and both women nodded.

"Yes, the money is there if you decide to proceed. Otherwise we will surrender it back to the foundation that pledged it to us."

"Thank you. We need to discuss all the details as a family before we can commit," María said as we shook hands and stood to leave. "But I'm also sure we'll take you up on it."

Justin

THE WEEKS flew by after we formally accepted the grant. By some miracle, along with long days of hard work from every single member of the family, we held our grand opening of López's Grocery and Butcher Shop over Labor Day weekend.

Moving the butcher shop from Northport to Wilcox went as planned. Other than a few folks disgruntled about the relocation, we expected to see the majority of our old customers at the new place, if word of mouth was any indication.

As for the grocery side, we all agreed it made the most sense for Cassie, who had a degree in business management, to step into the store-manager role. With her and María keeping us on track, we cleaned, ordered supplies, stocked the shelves, processed the meat, and moved the butcher shop—all in eight short weeks.

Amid the frenzy, there wasn't much time for Manuel and me to slip away to our secret love nest, which was no secret at all. Cassie found out the week after María, and then the rest of the family began treating it like Manuel and I were already living together.

Of course, Antonio considered the apartment his new after-school hangout, and by that, I mean he ate whatever food we had in the refrigerator. I swear the only thing keeping that kid lean and muscular was genetics.

Finally, after he cleaned me out of a peach cobbler I'd made for me and Manuel, I locked him out of the apartment and marched him downstairs to Cassie. "This one needs a job."

"What?" he asked, indignant. "I work for Mom."

"You do, and now you work for your aunt Cassie too," María said as she came into the grocery from the butcher shop. Whether or not she'd overheard my grumbling about her teenager having eaten me out of house and home, or simply figured additional responsibility would do him good, I wasn't sure.

"Mamá," he began to whine, and I had to look away to keep from laughing. Antonio could be too much, but I adored the crap out of him. His mom was no-nonsense. He needed to be busy doing something besides getting into trouble, and apparently, going to school, working the farm, helping in the butcher shop, *and* playing soccer wasn't enough.

I had just finished that conversation when I walked up front to grab a soda. I still had several hours prepping food for the next day ahead of me and needed the caffeine pick-me-up.

"Justin?" I heard someone say behind me. I turned with a smile, thinking it was one of our old Northport customers. Instead, I found myself face-to-face with Donny's sister.

"Margaret!" I exclaimed and pulled her in for a hug. "Oh my God, what brings you all the way to Wilcox?"

For a moment she looked pleased to see me, but her mouth turned down when she looked around the store. "Um, I-I heard you own this now."

I could feel her pain and, like a ton of bricks, I realized why she'd come. Donny died almost exactly a year ago, on September thirteenth. I'd already thought about the upcoming anniversary of that awful day and had begun emotionally preparing myself.

"Margaret, where are you staying?" I asked instead of answering about the store.

"Um, I'm planning to stay at a hotel in Roseburg. I didn't want to impose on you."

"There is no imposition. Are your bags in your car?" She nodded, confused. "Come with me. I have the perfect place for you to stay."

She led me to her rental car, and we drove to the back of the grocery store, then took the exterior staircase up to the apartment. I'd have to let everyone know I was letting her stay, but I knew no one would take issue with my hospitality.

"Wow, this is… maybe too much. Seriously, Justin, I—"

"Margaret, I'm happy you came, and of course, you're welcome to stay with me. This is currently unoccupied, and I'll be downstairs in the store most of the time if you need me."

At my words, her expression changed from surprise about the apartment to utter sadness. "Hey, you okay?" I asked. "Let's pull up a chair and you can tell me what's going on."

She nodded and followed me to the table for two. The moment we sat down, her tears began to flow. "We… um, *I* miss you. It's been a whole year since—"

I reached over and took her hand. "It's been a hard year for me too."

"You stopped texting."

I nodded and swallowed around a lump in my throat. "I figured it'd be easier on everyone, including me, if I disappeared. Your family… well, they wanted to forget I was in Donny's life, even while he was still with us."

"They regret how they treated you."

I snorted before I could help myself. "Margaret, you know I love ya, but I don't buy that."

She sighed. "It's true. When you left, they found this," she said, pulling a photograph out of her purse and handing it to me. I recognized the picture of Donny and me, sitting together in the very combine that killed him. I was straddling him like I used to do, my head thrown back in a laugh as he tickled me. Ben had captured the shot on his phone and printed it for Donny and me on Valentine's Day.

Ben hadn't reached out following Donny's death—not one text or call. I only texted Margaret for a few months after moving back to Oregon, but phones work both ways. But in a strange way maybe their radio silence had helped me heal. I'd found the support and love I needed within my family, old and new—my uncles, the Lópezes, Manuel.

I stared at the picture for a long moment. The tears that stung my eyes didn't fall. Instead, anger filled me. I wanted to lash out at Donny's greedy father for putting him in such a precarious position. The man knew the extreme danger of trying to harvest so close to the ravine. Yet the mighty dollar was more important than his son's safety, and that gamble cost Donny his life. *Our life.*

At the risk of crumpling the photograph in my fist, I set it back on the table and looked at Margaret. "This is hard to look at."

"You don't love him any longer?"

Her words stung like a slap across the face. "Margaret, why would you say that?"

"Because I heard you have someone new. It's only been a year, Justin. Couldn't you have waited?"

I stared at her, my mouth hanging open. "Waited for what? Suicide? I was close, Margaret, too close for too many months. Donny was my entire life, and I spent so much time wallowing in such depths of despair. Should I still be there? Would my misery make you feel better?"

I got up to leave, but she stood too. "I shouldn't have come. I won't need to stay here, Justin. I just came to see how you were doing. I can understand now why you no longer text."

I watched her leave, even slamming the door behind her. I didn't follow. Instead I slumped back into the chair and let the tears I'd been holding flow.

Pulling my phone out, I texted María, asking her to get the new employee I'd been training to finish prepping food for the butcher shop tomorrow.

I locked both doors and went back to the bedroom, crawled into a ball, and sobbed. It'd been a couple of months since I'd stopped thinking of Donny every day. Sometimes that made me feel guilty, but I figured it was natural. I'd convinced myself that Donny wouldn't want me to be miserable.

But seeing Margaret get so angry was a gut punch. Maybe I shouldn't have allowed myself to get involved with Manuel so soon after Donny's death. Maybe she was right to be angry.

I ignored Manuel's texts asking if I was okay. Most nights, I stayed at the house with Señor and Señora López, but tonight I needed alone time. I called Uncle Henry, told him what happened, and asked if I could stay there for a few nights. He agreed right away.

I texted María again to let her know I needed some days off and my replacement, who I'd been training, should be able to pick up the slack. I also let her know I'd be staying with my uncles, which I assumed would raise alarm bells through the grapevine, but I couldn't deal with that right now.

María: *Are you okay?*

Me: *No. That woman who approached me in the store was my late boyfriend's sister.*

María: *??*

Me: *Next week is the anniversary of his death.*

I didn't try to hide my emotions from my uncles. When I pulled myself out of my depression, I learned that I needed to let others in— my uncles especially, and eventually the López family. But right now I needed to process what happened with Margaret.

That meant taking a couple of days for myself, away from everyone. Fortunately, the grocery store and butcher shop would function fine without me. Cassie already ran the grocery side like a well-oiled machine, and the grant had afforded us the ability to train staff in all areas. What my trainee couldn't handle on the smoker, Carlos and Martín were more than capable of doing.

That night, after bear hugs from my uncles, I crawled into the bed that'd been my refuge time and again. I stared at the ceiling as Margaret's visit and the accusatory reaction to me seeing someone else "too soon" replayed on a loop in my mind. Eventually I fell asleep and dreamed of the day Ben took that picture on the combine.

I ended up taking more than a couple days off work. I found myself thrown back into the depression I hadn't felt since I faced the demon of the old farmhouse. I texted Manuel and asked him to give me space. Being such a kind, loving, considerate man, he did so, which only made me feel shittier for having asked.

I just needed to get through this anniversary and everything would be back to normal. But I wasn't sure if that was true or not. I wasn't even sure I knew what "normal" meant for me anymore.

Manuel

I DIDN'T PAY much attention to the fact that Justin didn't text me back right away, at least until María told me that the sister of Justin's late boyfriend had shown up. Then I realized it must've gone badly, because he'd retreated to his uncles' place.

"Should we move out of the house?" Mamá asked, her voice laced with concern, and I shook my head.

"No, not yet, Mamá. When I first met Justin, he was mourning the loss of his lover. It took a long time for him to let me in, for him to let any of us in. I'm sure he feels guilty, but let's give him time. He'll tell us what he needs when he's ready."

I hoped that was true, but it didn't mean my heart wasn't breaking. I was in love with Justin. My heart began to fall for him before he even gave the green light to an actual relationship. Now I wondered if the visit from Donny's sister would push us back to square one. Or maybe I'd lose him entirely.

I shook off that last thought as quickly as it appeared. My feelings for Justin—the love I felt for him—would never go away no matter what choices he made, no matter how much space and time he needed.

I was pleased that Henry and Jeff came over frequently to give us updates. With Justin's blessing, they recapped his conversation with Donny's sister and told us he'd broken down afterward and wasn't ready to face his new life again yet. That was a week ago, and I missed Justin with every ounce of my being.

My parents were tense. Of course, it was easy to forget they had uprooted their lives to move here with us. They were worried about the housing situation, which had to feel rather precarious right now. I had already looked for and found a small camper I could pull up to our house. If Justin needed his farmhouse back, my parents could move into either the camper or my room.

It wouldn't be ideal, but it'd work. "We are built of strong stuff," Papá had said all my life. "We will survive no matter where the current flows."

My heart, not so strong. Already I was mourning Justin's loss. I wasn't sure how I'd survive if he dumped me now. I couldn't just throw away the love I had for that man, but I would respect his wishes, and I would learn how to live with a heart that no longer beat.

I couldn't blame Justin if he decided it was too much. I went into our relationship with eyes wide open. I'd been fully aware of what he was going through when we met. Yet I pushed things. I made it clear I wanted more, and he relented. Now he was dealing with all the loss but couldn't or wouldn't reach out to me for comfort, not even as a friend. I should've given him more time.

María and Cassie, who'd both laid eyes on Donny's sister in the store, said they hadn't seen the woman again. I wondered if she was still in town or messaging Justin, making him feel bad about his relationship with me. Was she making him feel bad about his relationship with all of us?

I hoped not. Even if Justin and I didn't work out, I wanted him to have my family. They loved him as much as I did, albeit in a different way. I knew they would stay by his side if he let them. That's just the kind of people they are... *we* are. We are loyal, loving, and dedicated to those we consider ours.

Justin would devastate us all.

Justin

EVERYONE LET me be while I worked through all the emotions Margaret brought up. I beat myself up over not grieving long enough and redefining my world so soon after losing Donny.

I second-guessed my decision to renovate the farmhouse and invest Donny's life insurance into the business with the López family. I was second-guessing everything, especially my relationship with Manuel.

When my phone rang the day after Donny's death anniversary, I picked it up, knowing it was Margaret. "You hurt me, Justin," she said without saying hello. "I came out there to check on you and make sure you were okay. Then I find that you have a new boyfriend. New family. New business. Did you use Donny's money for that?"

The fire inside me began to burn when she laid into me for deserting her family. For half an hour, Margaret ripped me up one side and down the other, and the longer she did, the hotter I blazed inside.

"What? You've got nothing to say for yourself?" she yelled into the phone when she finally noticed I hadn't responded.

I took a moment to catch my breath before I unleashed on her. "Donny brought me home on Christmas, remember? It was snowing, and we were excited to have a white Christmas. Your mom said you hadn't had one in years. That night, your mother handed me her phone and said I needed to take a picture of *your* family. It was her way of telling me I wasn't part of it. To this day, you won't find a single photograph of us all together because there are none. That's not by accident, Margaret."

My heart was hammering, and I took a deep breath to calm myself down before I continued. "Donny and I graduated that May and decided to move in together. Remember Donny and I had jobs lined up? Then your father got sick. Had to have a stent, correct? Your mother called and asked Donny to come home. He could live in your grandparents' old house, and they'd fix it up for him. So we gave up the new jobs. Donny came home to help with the farm, which he wasn't in line to inherit since your *other* brother was the firstborn. Remember how your father made that clear after we'd given up our lives to help? Oh, and Margaret, do you remember how your brother told Donny I wasn't invited to the family reunion the following summer because it would upset your elderly family members?"

I didn't wait for her to answer. "I stayed with Donny even though your family was toxic, not just to me, but to him—the guy who'd sacrificed his entire life for all of you. I stayed because Donny's heart was so beautiful. I stayed because I loved him." Tears streamed down my face then, but I wasn't done. I knew I needed to get all this off my chest before it consumed me.

"None of you ever loved Donny like he deserved. None of you ever appreciated what an amazing person he was. I know, Margaret, because no one in your family could've hurt me if they'd known or cared that Donny loved me unconditionally. I will never forgive your father's greed and relentless desire to make, what, fifty bucks by farming so close to that ravine. I will never forgive your family for what they took from me, for sacrificing Donny on that goddamned combine. And I'll never understand why. Why did Donny push himself for a family who couldn't even open their lives to his partner? Why couldn't any of you welcome me into your hearts as another son, another brother? That's what I could've been, Margaret, but instead, you lost us both."

I should've hung up. I could hear Margaret's choked sobs and knew I'd spoken a truth she hadn't come to terms with. But she needed to hear it. She'd accused me of replacing Donny, and I wouldn't let that stand.

"I haven't forgotten your brother. He will always live in my heart. But I had to leave Iowa. I had no support there, no connections, no family. Your family forced me out of our home less than a week after I watched my beloved's body laid into the earth. Leaving is what I had to do to survive, and it's not the first time. My own father abused me, and then I became a victim of your family. I'm tired of being a victim, Margaret. I denounced it and dared to stand on my own two feet. Yes, I've met a new man, a good man. He'll never replace Donny, not that he's ever tried to. If anything, the love that man has shown me, *and* his family has shown me, has done nothing but accentuate the incredible life I had with your brother."

Silence lingered on the line, both of us sniffing. My cracked-open heart began to heal then, and the gaping rift I'd always felt between Donny's family and me had closed some. "I was so blessed to have

Donny in my life," I said so quietly it was almost a whisper. "He will always be in my heart, but by some miracle, I've been blessed again. Only this time, it comes with an entire package of people who care about me. I don't owe you or your family any explanation. Despite everything, I loved you and thought of you as a sister. I never thought you capable of putting anyone through what you've put me through these past few days. I hope you can find a way through your grief, Margaret, but please don't contact me again."

When I hung up, a sense of peace fell over me. I didn't need Margaret's approval. I didn't need anyone's approval for my own happiness. I spent the rest of the afternoon crying, but it felt cathartic. I'd finally purged Donny's toxic family from my life, and it freed up space in my mind and heart for his memory.

Tomorrow was Sunday, and I'd be damned if I didn't show up for family dinner at the López house. It was time to tell these wonderful people how much they meant to me.

Manuel

WHEN I CAME down the stairs and found Justin helping in the kitchen, I almost burst into tears. I'd missed him so much that my heart felt like it would explode at the sight of him.

I didn't know how he felt about me, and I didn't want to make him uncomfortable. So I headed for the front door, climbed onto the ATV, and rumbled across the pasture to check on the fences the elk loved to destroy. We'd finally replaced the wire with a cattle gate, but I needed an excuse not to be in the house until dinnertime.

The fencing remained intact, so I drove to the barn and checked on the hay. It'd been too dry for it to be dangerous, but hay stored wet could decompose, cause combustion, and burn the entire barn down. So, dry or not, I still needed to check.

When Papá walked from Justin's farmhouse and gestured to a couple of square bales for us to sit, I did as instructed.

"Are you okay, hijo?" he asked.

"Of course, Papá, why wouldn't I be?"

"Because your boyfriend has been gone for over a week, and when you finally saw him, you lit out of there like your ass was on fire."

I gave a wet chuckle, then eyed him suspiciously. "That may be true, but how do you know that? You and Mamá haven't left for dinner yet."

"Hijo, nothing happens that the women in this family don't know about. María heard you come downstairs but didn't see you, and then the front door shut. She figured you made a run for it and texted your mamá, who told me to be on the lookout for you."

I smiled sadly. "María. Of course. I did leave without saying hello. I didn't want to make Justin uncomfortable."

"What about you, hijo? Is it okay for you to be uncomfortable?"

I shook my head. "Papá, he has lost so much."

"And how will *you* feel if you lose him?"

I wasn't ready to face that question, not out loud, so I stood, ready to leave. "I'm sorry, Papá, I need—"

"You need to sit down and listen to me, hijo," he said as he pulled me back down onto the hay. "I am not upset with your Justin for being sad. *Mi madre* was devastated when Papá died, and he was a mean old rooster. She didn't talk for six months but got up daily and helped her family because you can't stop living. Being sad isn't a reason to throw people out of your life, especially if those people love you."

"He's still grieving, and we moved too fast. It's too soon."

"This is not a real thing, too soon. Love doesn't pay attention to time. The heart wants what it wants, hijo. If you love that boy, you must tell him. You must stand beside him even if he doesn't speak for six months. You stand with him, show him you love him, because when the clouds disperse, the sun will shine again. He will need his loved ones most when he is unable to give much back. Mamá was a good woman, hijo, as you know. She helped raise you and your brothers. If we'd turned away from her when she needed us most, we'd never have known how much love she was able to show us in her last days. Do you understand?"

"Papá, what if he doesn't want me?"

"Has he given almost everything he owns to this family, including the roof over our heads and his life savings, or was Carlos exaggerating?"

I sighed and looked away as a tear slipped down my cheek. "No, Papá, he did."

"Then he will want you."

"I'm not sure I can watch him love another."

Papá shrugged. "Manuel, that boy loves you. He's confused, and he may be too quiet sometimes about his emotions. Not everyone can be a hot Latin lover like us. But he shows his love in what he does. He works long hours, not just at the store but at home. He helps your mamá and María. He even helps to keep my wild grandson in order."

We both chuckled at that. "He looks at you like a big present sitting under a Christmas tree. When he doesn't think we're looking, he leans on you ever so slightly, and both your mamá and I have noticed that you seem to melt when he does. Not many people have that kind of relationship. It's special. He will see that when his heart stops hurting," Papá said. Then he gave my shoulder a squeeze.

I nodded and looked down. I hated getting emotional, and although Papá had never told me not to cry, I still felt like I shouldn't cry in front of him.

If he kept talking about what I felt and feared in my relationship with Justin, I'd lose all my cool and the tears would flow like a fountain.

Papá patted my knee, stood up, and slipped out of the barn. I stayed there thinking about what he'd said. He wasn't wrong. I remembered my abuela's quiet time, as we'd called it back then, the time she needed to heal from losing our abuelo. When she finally came out of it, she was still broken, but she was instrumental in helping to raise us—especially Martín and me. She also kept a watchful eye on Carlos, who was a teenager in love with a very rowdy young woman named María.

I took three long, deep breaths and let them out slowly. Papá was right. Justin needed me to stand by him. I'd already committed to giving him space if he needed it, but I'd let my fear keep me from seeing what my amor needed right now.

So I stood up, dusted off my jeans, and returned to the house. I went upstairs, showered like I always did before family meals, put on the cologne I wore anytime I was going to see my man, and made myself presentable.

When I came downstairs, I caught Justin's eye. In my mind, I said, *I'm here for you, mi amor, for whatever you need. I'm here.* He stared at me, a bit perplexed, but then gifted me with a smile as if he had heard what I tried to convey through my eyes. I returned his smile, and he disappeared back into the kitchen.

Then I sat down at the dining table next to Papá, who winked at me. How was I this old and still needed my father to put me on the right path? I was lucky to have him in my life.

Justin

I HEARD THE stairs creak and the front door shut and felt my heart drop. That had to be Manuel; he was the only one upstairs. I'd done wrong by not contacting him, and now he was avoiding me.

"Don't worry about him," María said as I sighed deeply.

"I'm so sorry, María. I-I fell apart."

"You can clear it up with him later. Now Mamá López wants to see if you remember what she taught you about *tres leches*."

I chuckled. "You're just trying to get my mind off all this, but I appreciate it."

María patted my back, then stationed me off to the side to make the cake. I'm not sure how I became the de facto dessert maker, but it felt good to have my own niche.

"Where's Cassie?" I asked when I noticed her absence.

"Not feeling well," María said brusquely. Judging by her tone and unusually stiff posture, I knew she was keeping something from me. I certainly wasn't dumb enough not to know what.

"She's pregnant?" I said, and she whirled around, mock-slapping at me.

"Hush, you aren't supposed to know."

I just laughed. "María, how can I not know? Cassie has been sick a lot, even before I… fell apart, and now she's missing a Sunday dinner? Oh, and your mother-in-law is mysteriously missing as well?"

María just grinned. "Well, keep your intuition to yourself. They don't want people to know yet." Her face grew solemn. "She's having some difficulties, and the doctors are concerned she might not be able to carry the baby to term."

I sighed and let it out slowly. "Oh, that's… well, that's scary. What did the doctors say?"

"That she needs to take it easy. If she can get through the first trimester, her chances are better."

Cassie was young, which worked in her favor. She was strong and healthy too. I'd once seen her pick up an entire side of beef and move it onto the table for Martín or Carlos to cut up. I hoped managing the grocery hadn't been an added strain. I was sure we'd need to talk about that soon, but not tonight.

María and I worked in silence to prepare dinner. When I heard Manuel come back into the house, slam the front door, and tear up the creaky stairs, I noticed María was conspicuously avoiding eye contact. I had a lot to clear up with him... with the whole family, really.

Tonight after dinner, when I explained things, I thought everyone would understand. I hoped they would, at least.

When dinner was ready, María called everyone into the dining room just as Señora López, Cassie, and Martín entered the house. "Good. Martín, come help Justin set three more places at the table," María demanded.

Martín smiled sweetly at his wife, went to the buffet, and began to pull out the dishes. Señora López went into the living room with Cassie, and a few moments later, I heard the TV turn off, and Carlos and Antonio showed up to help shortly after. By help, I mean they left the living room to avoid the sharpness of Señora López's tongue while she was in "protect her daughter-in-law" mode.

That drove home the difference between my new family and Donny's anything-but-supportive family.

I sat next to Manuel, as I always did, but he didn't do his usual lean-in or the sweet nudges I was used to. The absence of that caused my heart to crack in several places, and I was committed to doing what I could to have that back again.

The food was excellent, as usual, if more sparse than other meals I'd had with the family. Now that Señora López and Cassie wouldn't be as active in the kitchen, I needed to make sure María knew I was good for more than making dessert.

Once we finished the meal and before anyone could launch into discussions of this week's business, I stood up to get everyone's attention.

"I want to explain why I've been absent this past week and a half," I said.

"There is no need, Justin...." María began to say.

"There is. It's important I say this. My absence coincided with the first anniversary of my late boyfriend's death in a farming accident. You may not know that I was in a very dark place when I returned home to Oregon. It took months for me to function properly again, and then when I ran into Manuel and Antonio on the farm, I was facing a very dark period from my childhood. I was messed up when you all came into my life."

I paused and took several deep breaths. "I'm not going to go into detail about my past except to remind you that my old farmhouse was tainted with bad memories. When you combined that with the loss of a very good man, who I loved with all my heart, I... I was broken."

I looked around the room as heads nodded in understanding. Manuel stared at his clasped hands, showing me just how hard he was taking this.

"Manuel put the light back into my life. Slowly, and simply by being the sweet, gentle, and thoughtful man he is, he showed me there was still happiness to be found—even in Wilcox, even in my old, decaying farmhouse. Then he introduced me to his amazing family, all of you, who've embraced me and made me part of your circle."

I glanced around the room, looked into the eyes of every single person but Manuel, and willed myself not to get emotional. "Not once did you make me feel less-than. You never questioned my motives or condemned me or Manuel for who we are. Instead, you tried to steal my food," I said, gently swiping Antonio's shoulder and getting a chuckle out of him and the rest of the family. "You have become my family. I-I didn't have that with Donny's. They were not good people. When the only person in Donny's family who was ever nice to me showed up and made me feel guilty for finding love again, I fell back down that dark hole. It took me all this time to climb out."

I took another deep breath, let it out slowly, and continued. "Now that I'm on this side of the darkness, back in the light, I just wanted to tell you how grateful and proud I am to have all of you in my life." I rested my hand on Manuel's shoulder, and he finally looked up. "Thank you, each of you, for making me feel so loved."

I closed my eyes and gave myself a moment to get my emotions under control. When I opened them again, I smiled. "Now, who wants pastel de tres leches?"

Señor and Señora López reached over and squeezed my hands after I sat down. "You are welcome, hijo. You are and always will be part of us."

When I noticed every head around the table nodding, even Antonio, I couldn't hold the stupid tears back. I laughed it off as best I could when one rolled down my cheek before I could stop it. "Thanks, everyone, but for real, I want cake. All this emotional stuff has made me crave sugar."

Once everyone had been served—by Carlos and Martín this time—Manuel leaned over and nudged me. "You okay?" he asked quietly.

"I'm better than okay, now that I'm here with all of you," I whispered back.

Manuel nodded, then dug into his cake. When he smiled, I knew I'd finally gotten the recipe right. "This is very good," he announced.

"I guess I just had to have big emotions to get it right."

Both María and Señora López laughed. "Food always tastes better when made with emotion, Justin," María said. I had to agree.

Manuel

JUSTIN AND I walked in silence along the worn path between his house and our family home. The heat had finally broken after the hot, dry summer. A gentle breeze blew through the grass, which, thanks to another rain, was tall enough for another haying this year.

Justin took my hand as soon as we were on the side of the hill, looking down into the valley where his house stood. "I-I'm sorry I went MIA," he said.

I squeezed his hand and then pulled him to my side. We stopped and gazed out across the beautiful expanse. It'd always been my favorite part of the property. Justin's land started down the hill from here and encompassed the entire valley. Before we released the cows back into his pastures, it was overgrown, but now that we'd mowed down all the brush and the cows had done their best to keep the grass managed, it was a stunning view from up here.

I'd spent a lot of time looking at that tiny home in the valley, thinking about the remarkable man I was now holding next to me. "I was worried, Justin. I-I thought you might be done with me."

He nodded but didn't respond right away. Instead, he snuggled deeper. Finally, after a long moment, he sighed and asked, "Manuel, have you ever lost someone really important to you?"

I thought of my abuela and nodded. "Yes, my grandmother."

"Did you ever feel guilty that you were replacing her?" he asked.

I shook my head. "No one could replace mi abuela. She was fierce."

Justin chuckled. "I'm sure that's true, after meeting your parents, but I guess you've never had to face the same loss as me. Your abuela just was and always would be your grandmother. So many emotions are wrapped up in my Donny. We never married. I met him as an eighteen-year-old college freshman, and we dated for years. He was my first real boyfriend. Can you imagine that?" he asked, chuckling.

"After we graduated, we moved onto his parents' farm, and they weren't exactly open-minded. Donny was never comfortable taking our relationship to the next level and getting married, even though we were fully committed to each other. But legally, and as far as his parents were concerned, our relationship could've ended at any moment. And that's exactly what happened. When Donny died, I was tossed out of the home shortly after they put him into the ground. Treated like just some renter being evicted rather than practically a son-in-law."

Justin was silent for a long stretch, studying the landscape. Finally he turned to face me. "Margaret, Donny's sister, was the only person in his family who cared about us. She'd come by when she was home from Chicago, and we'd sit out on the back porch and laugh about the shenanigans she and Donny got up to as kids. As a result, I thought of her as family. Someone important. Besides Donny and my uncles, I didn't have anyone. That's why when she came here and yelled at me for not mourning Donny like she thought I should, it sent me back over the edge."

When he held my gaze, I wondered if he wanted me to understand something I was missing. He shook his head then and said, "Manuel, Margaret called and yelled at me again yesterday, and something broke inside. I began to see Donny's family for who they really are. Donny loved me, there is no doubt in my mind, but he never fought for me. In a way, he let his family kill him. As I was listening to Margaret, angry that I'd found peace around Donny's loss—all while not putting responsibility for his death on her greedy father—and at their treatment of me after he was gone, I saw the difference between him and you. I don't mean to compare, but it's hard not to. Your family has made me feel a part of them since I stumbled into their lives. That's so important to me, but what matters even more is that I've fallen for them and you. I can see a life together with you, and when I think about that, I see your big, unruly family as part of the vision. I know that probably sounds crazy, but—"

I cut off his rambling with a gentle kiss, then released his lips just as quickly. As bad as I wanted to deepen the kiss, hashing out our feelings took top priority right now. "Justin, it doesn't sound crazy, it sounds right. You... you're the most right person for me that I've ever met. I care about you so much it makes my heart ache. I'm in love with you."

Shimmering eyes met mine, and a look of joy mixed with relief crossed Justin's face. "Manuel, that's exactly how this feels to me too. I love you so much it hurts my insides... but when that hurt rubs up against my other hurts, it can become overwhelming. That's when I retreat."

I nodded, thinking he was telling me he needed me to back off, but he continued. "I'm tired of letting that overwhelming feeling keep me from having this." He waved a finger between us. "I want all of this, okay? I want all of you."

I couldn't help the happiness that engulfed my entire body at hearing him say that. "I want all of this too, Justin—the good and the bad, the easy times and the difficult. I can be a safe space for you, always, if you'll let me."

I wrapped him in my arms and kissed him with everything I had. When I pulled back, he was smiling. "Ready to move in with me now?" he asked.

"Oh yeah, the apartment?" I asked, and he smiled.

"Our own little love nest."

"Let's go test it out right now, shall we?"

Justin

"MR. LATHAM?" the caller asked.

"Yes, this is him," I said, rolling my eyes at what I assumed was a sales call.

"Hello, I'm Clarence Jacobs. I'm the attorney for the Dougherty family."

My spine stiffened. Donny's family was coming after me now? I was about to tell the man he needed to speak with my uncle before I could say something to incriminate myself when he cleared his throat and continued.

"I've been asked to contact you regarding the late Donald Dougherty's estate."

"There wasn't an estate," I said. "Donny and I lived on his parents' farm. We didn't own any property or the house we occupied. Nothing."

"Well, that's not exactly true about nothing. Donny was the beneficiary of a trust established by his grandparents, and you were named as the sole heir in his will. So you inherited the trust."

"What? I-I've never heard of this."

"It's possible Mr. Dougherty didn't realize he stood to benefit from it. The trust fund wasn't due for distribution until he turned twenty-five."

"But Donny had a will?"

"Yes, he set that up with me, Mr. Latham, when you moved to his parents' farm. It wasn't until last week that I learned you hadn't received anything he'd left you in the will. I apologize for that. The Dougherty family had assured me that Donny's belongings had been given to you."

I let out a bitter laugh. "You were told wrong, Mr. Jacobs. Their parting gift to me was kicking me out of the home I shared with Donny and threatening to have the sheriff forcibly remove me if I tried to stay."

The attorney sighed. "Again, Mr. Latham, I'm very sorry. Donny didn't own the home, but he did have around ten thousand dollars in his savings account. I've already alerted the sheriff that the family appears to have stolen that from you."

"How… how did you find all this out?" I asked.

"When I alerted Donny's siblings that their trust funds were ready to be distributed, Margaret informed me that she was suspicious that her brother may have collected Donny's money rather than send it to you as promised. I understood she was coming to meet with you to discuss that in person."

"Oh, she did visit, but we got into an argument," I said, realizing now why things had gone down so incredibly bad. "She didn't mention the money."

"Again, I'm very sorry, Mr. Latham, but I assure you, I will do what I can to hold Mr. Dougherty accountable. In the meantime, you are the heir to around three hundred fifty thousand dollars. I will need to meet with you to discuss how that will be distributed."

The amount shocked me so much, I had to sit down. "Okay," I managed to mumble before I regained my composure. "Do you think I'll have problems with Donny's family over all this? Things were bad enough before when money *wasn't* a factor."

"Either of his siblings could dispute the will. However, since there is theft and possibly fraud involved in withholding Donny's estate from you, I'm guessing they'll be less likely to pursue it. I would recommend you proceed sooner rather than later in claiming your inheritance, though. When can you come to my office?"

I laughed and told him I lived in Oregon now, but gave him Uncle Henry's number and asked him to set up arrangements for us to work through all the legal stuff remotely.

Three hundred fifty thousand dollars. No wonder Margaret had shown up out of the blue. I guess that explained why she was so angry too, to some extent. Maybe she felt I didn't deserve it after she learned I had created a good life for myself without her brother. Knowing now that Donny's older brother had stolen money from me, ignoring Donny's final wishes in the process, made me wish I could have another go at that family.

I quickly called Uncle Henry, but his line was busy, so I assumed he was talking to the attorney. Financially, we were well set up with the grocery store and butcher shop business. I'd used Donny's life insurance money to cover those expenses and fix up the old farmhouse.

To find out he had a trust fund was overwhelming, and the weirdest thing was that Donny didn't even know he did that for me. Even in death, married or not, he had taken care of me. I wondered if he made me his sole heir in his will because deep down he knew his parents and siblings would turn on me.

I needed to figure out what to do with the nest egg. I wanted to do something in Donny's name. He deserved to be remembered for being the amazing human being he was, but I'd have to think about the best way to honor him.

Uncle Henry called a few minutes later and told me he'd spoken with the attorney from Iowa. "What the hell, Justin? Who were these people?"

"Just homophobic assholes, nothing new or special about them."

"Well, according to this Clarence Jacobs, the law is about to come down on them hard. Anyway, sounds like you're about to come into some money. Are you okay? It's got to be quite the surprise."

"Yeah, I'm still in shock. I'm grateful to Donny and angry at his family, but mostly I'm sad. He was too good for them, and they keep finding ways to prove that."

"How about you come over for lunch? Your uncle Jeff and I would like to spend some time with you."

I thought about everything I needed to do at the store and all the mixed-up emotions I needed to somehow sort through. But I'd spent enough time wallowing in self-pity. I had zero desire to go back down that dark hole. "Yeah, let me check in with María and Cassie. If they've got everything under control, I'll come over."

"Great. See ya in a bit, son," he said and hung up.

As usual, my uncles were who I needed to help get my head on straight. For the first time since Donny's death, I also knew that while I processed all that'd happened, I'd have my sweet Manuel to support me too.

I was blessed.

Manuel

"WE'RE EXPECTING!" Martín announced at our Sunday family dinner.

"Really?" I asked, pretending I didn't know. Poor Martín and Cassie. We all knew, even Antonio, who was clueless when it came to family dynamics. But I didn't want to dim their big reveal, so I went along with the "surprise" announcement.

"We're going to have a March baby!" Cassie said, beaming.

Justin hugged them both and then rushed into the kitchen, brought back a piece of chocolate cake, and placed it in front of the soon-to-be parents.

"So, we have a huge request," Cassie said, looking at Justin as he sat down with a piece of cake for himself. He cocked an eyebrow when it became clear she was stalling. "You can say no if you want to, but—"

Cassie looked over at her husband, who shrugged. "We want to move into the apartment above the grocery store," Martín said. "Cassie can't be doing a lot of back-and-forth, and she wants to stay on as the manager. Being on-site would make it easier on her physically, especially if things pop up when she's not on duty."

Justin stared at them, listened without giving anything away, then looked at me. I could tell he was trying not to be upset about possibly losing our love nest, just as we'd reclaimed it for ourselves. "Um, well, we were going to move in there, Justin and me," I quickly said to keep the heat off him.

"I don't think that's going to be a problem," María said. "Mamá and Papá López have agreed to move in here with us because"—she smiled at Carlos, and he winked in reply—"we're expecting as well."

That news did surprise me. María had complications when she had Antonio. Then, because of fibroids that were causing her a lot of pain, she'd had one ovary removed. We all thought that meant no more nieces or nephews from her and Carlos.

"Are you sure you're okay?" I asked, suddenly concerned having another baby might be dangerous for her health. "Have you got a doctor monitoring everything?"

She shrugged. "Officially, they consider it a geriatric pregnancy, since I'm in my mid-thirties, but I've been assured by the doctor in town that it's not uncommon these days. They will have to keep an eye on me and the baby."

"Cassie, you and María are going to be pregnant at the same time. Wow," Justin said.

"Si Dios quiere," Papá said.

"God willing, indeed," I said. "Well, things are about to get interesting around here. María, when are you due?"

She smiled. "Around June."

"Then it's definitely God's will," I replied to the chuckles of the group.

"As is Justin having his home back," Mamá said, then winked at me.

I blushed because that statement contained a few inferences that I didn't want to discuss with my parents.

I sat back and listened as my family talked over one another, discussing the pregnancies and how the cousins would grow up together. I glanced over at my nephew, whose face was full of wonder. That was good. At sixteen, he wasn't feeling replaced. The fact that his birthday was about the same time made me wonder if he would think of his little sibling as his gift. That thought made me happy.

When Justin's hand slipped into mine, I raised it to my lips to kiss. It had been a great day. Our family was expanding. The conversation later turned to living arrangements, with Mamá and Papá planning to move into Cassie and Martín's room on the first floor of the house. It wasn't as big as the master bedroom upstairs, but they could avoid the stairs.

"Are you okay giving up the apartment in the grocery store?" I whispered in Justin's ear.

He nodded. "Are you okay moving in with me?" he whispered back.

"Oh, you know I am," I said, louder than I intended, which got a chuckle out of him.

After the meal, Justin congratulated Cassie and told her his baby-shower gift was our love nest, and he could box up the keys if she felt the need to unwrap it at the baby shower.

She laughed and hugged him, then me. "Thank you so much. Seriously, though, can we move in this week?"

"Of course, and we'll help," he said, including me in the plans. That was the first time Justin had spoken for us, as a couple. I liked it but didn't say anything because I didn't want to make him self-conscious. I really did like where our lives were heading—together.

Justin

WITH THE holidays came an intensity at our store I wasn't fully prepared for. With Cassie and María pregnant and required to take it easy, Manuel, Martín, Carlos, and I were up to our ears in work. Even Antonio pulled extra shifts when he got out of school.

Not that I minded. I loved how well our little business was doing. Thank God the grant had come through during the summer and we had the funds to hire and train staff before the holidays. Even with a full roster, we worked overtime to keep the shelves stocked, the butcher supplied with cut meats, and the barbeque cooked and ready for customers.

We'd already torn out the up-front section that butted up against our butcher shop and where the cashiers checked people out. Originally, they'd served fried chicken and typical store-cooked foods there.

When we'd quickly outgrown the mini restaurant in the butcher shop. With the incredible barbeque and Mamá López's cooking, it made sense to use the space as a restaurant with seating for people who wanted to buy food from the smoker to eat there.

Luckily, converting the space didn't take much, since it was designed for that anyway.

I'd noticed that Señora López tired quickly the few days she'd put in long hours. I secretly thought she might like taking on a bakery area where she supplied desserts for the barbeque menu—nothing extreme, just simple fare that could be sold fresh daily.

Unfortunately, that idea had to be put on hold until María and Cassie were out of the woods. Señora López was understandably occupied keeping her daughters-in-law healthy and happy. And by that, I mean constantly fussing at them to take it easy. I was glad she was here, because none of us would've been brave enough to face down either of them with that recommendation, even if they both needed to be careful.

Manuel

By the time Christmas rolled around, we all needed a break. We worked Christmas Eve and had a skeleton crew until noon on Christmas Day, but we were all free to be together for a holiday dinner.

I hadn't officially moved in with Justin yet, although I spent every night at his place. Also, our family get-togethers were always at his house, since we had officially become boyfriends. His uncles joined us most Sundays too.

Mamá and María helped decorate his home for Christmas, which Justin seemed to love. Cassie was put on bed rest after she almost miscarried. Her pregnancy was so difficult that Martín took over her duties as store manager, and mostly, we left her to the apartment upstairs.

But that didn't mean she stopped managing altogether. With the curtains open, she could keep an eye on things without being down on the floor. Cassie had become quite the control freak since she'd become the boss lady of López's Grocery.

Justin's uncles arrived in the early afternoon and helped set the table. María refused to give up "her kitchen," as she called it, even when at Justin's house, and only slowed down when Mamá told her to step away for the baby's sake. Unlike Cassie, María didn't seem to have any problems carrying a little one. That just made it more difficult to convince her to rest.

When Martín and Cassie arrived, we gathered around the table, and Papá offered blessings over the feast. Justin and his uncles chatted about things happening in town, and Martín helicoptered over Cassie, which caused her to give him the stink eye. Papá and Carlos were arguing over who were the most promising soccer teams this year, and María and Mamá were discussing whether some spice tasted better cooked. They were farther away from me, so I could only catch the gist of the conversation. I glanced over at my nephew, who was texting while shoving food into his face. María told us last week that Antonio had met a girl he liked, so I assumed he was texting her.

My family. It made me feel utterly content watching them all together like this—getting along and genuinely enjoying each other's company.

When I turned toward Justin, he smiled at me, which always caused my heart to do a funny little blip. Then he went back to talking to his uncles.

I wonder if he'd say yes if I asked him to marry me, I thought. For a frightening moment, I thought about falling to one knee and asking him right then and there. Luckily I came to my senses when María, apparently having reached a stalemate in her argument with Mamá's about spices, got up and announced it was time for presents.

I'd bought Justin a painting by an El Paso artist whose work he liked. He'd seen her art at the festival when we went to pick up Mamá and Papá. The painting depicted a huge blue hummingbird drinking from a red flower. It was bold and beautiful and would look good displayed over Mamá's buffet, which now stood next to Justin's kitchen.

I glanced around at the family heirlooms that remained in the home with Justin and laughed to myself. We had completely taken over the poor man's home, and he didn't seem to mind. If he was to be believed, he loved it.

I had bought the painting before we left El Paso and asked the artist to mail it to us for Christmas. It may have been presumptuous to think Justin would want something like that from me at that stage of our relationship. Thinking back on it, though, maybe providence told me we would be closer at this point.

Or perhaps I should've bought him a ring instead of a painting. I very much wanted to propose tonight.

But it was too much, I knew he wasn't ready, and that was okay. We opened presents, and Justin *ooh*ed and *aah*ed over the painting and rushed to put it up in the space above the buffet. It fit perfectly there, just like I knew it would.

When he brought me a small gift, I almost freaked. It was the size of a ring box. Was he about to propose? Surely not. I opened the paper, and when I saw the beautiful gold chain with the cow horn pendant, I laughed and hugged him.

I'd lost my necklace somewhere on the farm when I was dumb enough to wear it while working. I'd lamented the loss, since it was a chain my abuelo had bought me before he died. The fact that Justin had thought to get that for me three months later and put the cow horns on it showed how much my man understood me.

Although, secretly, I'd have liked a ring even more. That could wait, though. Right?

That night, as I lay on the sofa with Justin in my arms and a crackling fire in the fireplace lulling us to sleep, I couldn't shake the question plaguing me all evening. "If I'd asked you to marry me tonight, would you have said yes?" I asked.

Justin sat up and locked eyes with me. "Were you considering it?"

I shook my head. "No, I mean, not tonight. It just came to me while we were sitting with the family. Tell me, though, would you have agreed?"

Justin shrugged, but his smile gave him away. "You might try actually popping the question and see what answer you get... but not for a while. Let's get through the baby season first, okay?"

I laughed. Cassie's and María's pregnancies were a lot. He was right. We didn't want to put more stress on the situation.

He also hadn't said no.

Justin

I LOVED LIVING with Manuel. I had stupidly discouraged him from proposing at Christmas. Jeez, what was I thinking? But times were already stressful, with the sisters-in-law being pregnant and everyone nesting and setting up their homes.

Mr. Jacobs had contacted Uncle Henry to say they'd arrested Donny's brother and wanted to know if I was pressing charges.

"No, I don't want anything to do with them. But he needs to pay me back every dime he stole. That wasn't his money, it was Donny's," I told Uncle Henry. The money from the trust-fund inheritance had come through as well, though I still felt unsure about it.

I had the money put into an interest-bearing account and left it there until I could figure out what to do with it. Using the funds in a way that honored Donny would require a lot of thought and planning, and I'd barely had time to think about it.

Life was continuing to come at us fast, so it was probably best that Manuel and I hadn't pushed things. That made sense, but I couldn't think of anything I'd like more than being married to him.

When I heard of the celebration in Eugene for Benito Juárez's birthday—a national holiday in Mexico—I got a bizarre idea, one that would involve more than just me. So I went searching for María in the butcher shop. We usually had a lull in customers around two in the afternoon, so I hoped I could get a moment alone with her.

Sure enough, the workers were busy preparing for the evening rush, and María was wiping down the counters and tables. I grabbed a washcloth and did the tables in the restaurant and then met her back in the store.

"What do you think about hosting a Juárez celebration here in March? Nothing big, just some barbeque and maybe live music on the lawn at the town hall."

"Really? Do you think they'd want that here?" María asked, sounding skeptical but curious.

"Probably. Everyone loves a good party. Besides, Wilcox could use a little cultural diversity. What do you think?"

She shrugged. "If you can get it set up in time, I'm guessing your Uncle Henry could talk to the mayor for you about event permits."

She was about to walk away when I said, "I think I'd like to propose to Manuel, and thought that might be the perfect venue."

María quickly turned back around. "Oh, if this is a romantic gesture, then yes, I'm all in."

For some reason, her sudden enthusiasm made me nervous. "Is it too much? I mean, Manuel told me he used to dance at the festival in El Paso. I-I just thought it'd be nice to have something special, something from home, happening when I, you know, ask him."

María laughed. "He would love that, and so would Mamá and Papá López. Here, come with me." She pulled me out of the butcher shop and up to Cassie and Martín's apartment. When she knocked, Señora López opened the door.

"What's going on?" she asked.

"We need to talk," María said, as she led me inside to sit at a table far larger than the one I'd had for Manuel and me.

"Justin thinks we should hold a town celebration for Benito Juárez's birthday."

"Oh, that sounds nice," Señora López said, smiling at me.

"He also wants to propose to Manuel while it's happening."

Señora López jumped up and clapped her hands together. "Oh, Justin, that's perfect. We wondered when you two might do that. Yes, this is wonderful news, but you don't need to hold a huge celebration for the asking. You boys getting engaged will be celebration enough."

She pondered, then tapped her tooth with her long fingernail. "We can do something special here in the restaurant, invite the mayor and city officials. We can have a maríachi band, if you want, and serve traditional Mexican food. Yes, let's keep it simple so when you're ready to propose, you can let *mijo* whisk you away, and you won't have to worry about party cleanup because *tu familia* will handle it."

"See, I knew Mamá López would know what to do," María said.

I chuckled. "Gracias, Señora López."

"No, no more of that. I'm Mamá López for you. You are going to be mi hijo, after all."

"And it'll be my honor, being your son," I said, and I got teary when I leaned over to hug her.

Only then did I notice someone conspicuously absent from our mini meeting. "How's Cassie?" I asked.

Mamá López shook her head. "She's in bed and still having contractions. I think we'll have to go to the hospital soon."

"Where's Martín?" María asked.

"He's downstairs on the phone with the doctor. He said the reception up here was bad, but I think he just wanted to speak with him without concerning her," she whispered so Cassie wouldn't hear.

"It's only four weeks early, though. That's not bad, right?" I asked, keeping my voice low.

Both women shrugged. "Est in manibus Dei," Mamá López said, and I knew she meant it was in God's hands now.

When Martín came in a few moments later, he looked serious. "We need to get her to the hospital," he whispered. "Justin, can we use your truck to get to Eugene? I don't trust mine or Manuel's, and they want us to go directly to the university hospital."

"Of course," I said and handed over my keys. When Martín brought Cassie out of the bedroom, it was obvious she wasn't doing well. My concern shifted to full-out worry.

"Um, let us know if you need anything." I wished I could hug Cassie, but it wasn't the time for that. Even getting her down the stairs to my truck was almost too much for her.

María and Mamá López went with them, and I hurried back into the store to let the staff know María wouldn't be back and that they'd taken Cassie to the hospital.

I quickly called Manuel and told him what was happening. "Sí, Mamá just called. I'm going to take Papá to the hospital too. Do you want to come with us?" he asked.

"Yes, but I think I better stay here in case I need to step in with Martín and María being out."

"Sí, makes sense," he said. "I'll call you when we know anything."

"Manuel, even if it's bad news, keep me informed. This is my family too," I said, quickly wiping a tear off my cheek.

"Es verdad, mi amor," he said and ended the call.

I was a nervous wreck, which made all of our employees nervous, so when no one needed me, I went to the freezers to stock up. Doing something productive helped distract me from my worry.

I got periodic text updates from Manuel. Mostly, the news was bad. They'd decided to do an emergency C-section when they saw the baby and Cassie were in distress. Cassie hadn't dilated enough, but the baby was… well, I didn't understand it all, just that it was a dire situation.

The store and shop were in good enough hands with our trusted employees that after the dinner rush, I walked over to my uncles' house, too nervous to be home alone. I paced their living room floor while they talked me down.

Finally, at eight fifteen, I got a call from a thrilled Manuel. "¡Mi amor! New mama and baby girl are both healthy and resting comfortably."

Tears burst free, and I had to sit down as my emotions got the better of me. "Thank God," I finally said. "I've been so worried, Manuel."

"We all were, Justin, but rest assured, they're fine. Baby Ana is so beautiful. I can't wait for you to see her."

"I'll come tomorrow. Are you coming home tonight?" I asked.

"Sí, our niece and her parents need to rest now. Carlos drove here and will take María and Mamá and Papá home. Do I need to pick you up since Martín brought your truck? You're still at your tíos' house, yes?"

I laughed, having forgotten I didn't have my own transportation. "Yes, if you don't mind. I'll see you when you get here," I said.

When I hung up, I put my head in my hands and let relief wash over me. I sighed when Uncle Henry's hand slid up and down my back. "It's amazing to see how much you love them," he said, and I looked up. "Yeah?"

He nodded, smiling. "I'm so happy you've found your footing, Justin. Do you know how you're feeling right now?" he asked as he sat across from me. I nodded. "When you see that baby tomorrow, your heart will grow to the size of Texas, and when it does, you'll understand how much your uncle Jeff and I love you."

I couldn't hold back a few more tears. "It's a lot of work to love people this much, huh?"

Uncle Henry shrugged. "Incredible, amazing, highly rewarding work."

Manuel

WE WERE all enamored of the adorable little girl snuggled into her papá's arms. Martín was as proud as a bantam rooster, strutting around or rushing to make sure his wife had everything she needed. And every chance he had, the new father held his daughter.

They tolerated our fussing over them for about a week before Cassie told us all she adored us but to get the hell out.

Even Mamá laughed. She kissed her, Martín, and the top of Ana's head, and then shooed us out of the little apartment.

"They will need time to nest now," Mamá said. Of course, there was plenty of work for the rest of us. Our heifers had begun having calves, so it didn't do for me to not be on the farm. But I figured the cows would be fine if I wasn't there from sunup to sundown like I would've been in the past. I had a niece to spoil, after all.

It took a while for things to get back to normal, both on the farm and at the store. When Cassie showed up downstairs with Ana strapped to her, it was obvious she was done being cooped up in that apartment. Nesting time was over.

She seamlessly resumed her role as store manager, and even though it'd only been a few weeks since she stepped back, it was noticeable that she was missed.

It wouldn't be long before she whipped things back into shape as she saw fit.

WEEKS PASSED, and I got home later than I wanted after driving to the farm's far side to search for one of our cows. She'd required help to deliver her calf last year, so I was trying to keep a close eye on her this time. But I found her lying under a tree with a couple of her besties, chewing her cud, happy and comfortable as can be.

When I drove up to the house on my ATV, hoping I hadn't completely missed Sunday dinner, I was pleased to see that the family had put up sparkly lights around the porch and pulled the table from the house so we could eat outside.

That, more than anything, reminded me of El Paso. Especially in the spring and fall, we'd gather outside in our courtyard and eat together.

When I walked in, María took one look at me and sent me to shower and clean up. "Don't come out here smelling like cows, and wear your date-night clothes," she said, referring to the nice shirt and jeans I only wore when going dancing at the community center with Justin.

I shook my head but did as I was told. I, like my sister-in-law, sometimes preferred to fancy up a little. The warm night was a good time to experience our Sunday dinner outdoors.

The family was all sitting around the table when I came down, and everyone stopped talking when they saw me. I cocked an eyebrow in question and noticed Justin's seat was empty. I was just about to sit down when I heard mariachi music and turned around to see a band coming around the corner of the house.

When Justin emerged from behind them, I stood watching, confused. "What's going on?" I asked, but besides a few snickers, no one answered.

When I noticed María and Cassie filming with their phones, I figured this would either be embarrassing or important.

When the band approached the side of the porch, still singing and playing, Justin stepped onto the porch and knelt in front of me.

My mouth dropped open as realization dawned. Then he turned his beautiful face up to me and held out a box with a ring inside. The band stopped playing, and Justin cleared his throat. "Manuel, I love you so much, so completely, I just couldn't wait any longer. You've become such an important part of my life. I wake up in the morning excited to see your face, and I go to bed at night so thankful to have your warm arms around me. I want to make this a lifetime commitment. Will you be my husband?"

I chuckled as happy tears rolled down both cheeks. I reached down, pulled my handsome boyfriend to his feet, and kissed him thoroughly, to the whoops and whistles of the family. "Yes, mi amor. More than anything in the world, I would love to be your husband. Yes!"

Epilogue:
Justin

THE WEDDING was going to be right here at the house, on the property that held so many negative memories just a year ago.

It had been transformed by the love and support of the incredible López family, but their healing power wasn't limited to the house. I had also grown as a person and healed from within because of their love and patient understanding.

Martín and Cassie were moving forward with plans to build a home in a picturesque area of the valley that overlooked the house I shared with Manuel. They said the apartment was great, but little Ana would eventually need her own space. Rhys, who did the stunning renovation of my home, was doing the work, and his stepfather was the architect.

When I volunteered Donny's money to pay for the new house, they refused, but I assured them it was the best way I could honor him. The money was depressing because of all that happened, so using it to directly benefit my family rather than myself felt right.

Even though I hadn't pressed charges, Donny's brother entered a plea for a lesser sentence and was now a convicted felon. Using the money at the center of all that nastiness to provide hearth and home for a happy, functional family—something Donny and I never had—was more than I could've dreamed for myself.

In many ways, I thought the love of the Lópezes was somehow healing Donny too. Maybe that was wishful thinking, but the thought gave me comfort.

Besides that, I donated a big chunk of the money to the college where Donny and I met. Every year, provided the interest continued to accumulate, the Donny Dougherty Scholarship would be offered to a student who needed assistance when their family either wouldn't or couldn't support them financially in their quest to earn a degree.

I'd been lucky because my uncles had contributed to fund my education. Donny's parents hadn't become the evil jerks they transformed into until later, but there were kids, especially LGBTQ kids, who found themselves without the support necessary to get through school.

Despite telling Margaret I didn't want her in my life, I was surprised to get a card from her in the mail, along with a picture of her and a stunningly beautiful woman.

Justin,

I wanted to apologize for what happened during my visit to Wilcox and the last time we talked. I was hurting over Donny, obviously, but that was no excuse for how I treated you.

Please know I've regretted that ever since you confronted me.

The reason I'm writing is to introduce you to Laura. She's the woman in the picture I've included with this card. Laura has been my lover for over six years. Mostly because of how my family treated you, I was too scared to let things progress with her.

When you laid things out so clearly, showing me how my family was not only responsible for the pain you felt over Donny's death but even for him being dead, I realized I had given them too much control over our lives.

Laura and I are engaged to be married. I know you don't want to see me again, but I'd love to have you come to our wedding. I would also like you to stand in for Donny and lead me down the aisle. Of course I would love nothing more than for you to bring the man who has helped heal your heart.

Both Laura and I would like to meet your Manuel.

I will send you a wedding invitation when we set a date, and I will understand if you decline, but please consider my request.

With great remorse and even greater love,

Margaret Dougherty

Margaret hadn't mentioned her brother's felony charge or the inheritance, but I couldn't blame her for not wanting to go there. Her letter touched my heart, but I wasn't committed to going to her wedding. That might be too much for me, but I was happy she'd asked.

I texted her the following week to congratulate her. I'd see how I felt about attending when the invitation came.

As part of a countywide effort to preserve the historical bridges around Wilcox, Xander McLeroy and his crew had restored the covered bridge next to my farm. The thing turned out beautiful, and with its elegant whitewashed walls and forest-green roof, it screamed the perfect wedding venue.

The bridge had been a refuge for me even before my father turned toxic. Admittedly, I hadn't spent much time on the bridge since I returned home. As it took on a new life thanks to Xander, I knew it was where I wanted to get married.

Of course, all I had to do was mention it to Xander, and he got the mayor involved. It was all planned out even before the park was officially dedicated. "You should be the first to use this bridge since you are its nearest neighbor," Mayor Polly insisted.

Manuel and I opted for an evening wedding, and couldn't have picked a better one for it. It was the end of June, so there was still plenty of light, but twinkle lights had been hung from the porch and the giant oak trees that dotted our front yard. A light breeze blew through the trees, making the twinkle lights dance and adding to the sound of the flowing creek below the bridge. It all felt so tranquil.

Cassie had taken charge of getting the bridge decked out for the wedding, and her décor only enhanced its elegance and ambiance. My soon-to-be sister-in-law might need to talk to our friends Declan and Pierce about becoming their business's wedding planner because she had a natural talent for it.

Manuel and I agreed to have a traditional wedding without writing our own vows. I often told him how much I cared about him, and I was sure he already knew.

Right before Mayor Polly, who had all but begged us to officiate the wedding, pronounced us husbands, Martín and Carlos stood up and brought a guitar to Manuel, who smiled and winked at me.

I'd been formally studying Spanish, and my course included listening to both traditional and modern music. I especially enjoyed the love songs, so I recognized "Nada Valgo Sin Tu Amor" by Juanes when Manuel began to sing. More than any other, that song encapsulated how I felt about him and his beautiful family and about what our wedding day meant to me and our future together.

When he sang the verse about standing next to me as the years passed, next to his family and friends, I felt María, my maid of honor, slip her arm around me.

She understood the significance of tonight and of officially becoming a member of this family. I now held the title of the newest López, though not by much, and I glanced at my uncle Jeff sitting in the front, holding my nephew, María and Carlos's newborn baby. Both the little one and Uncle Jeff appeared pleased to be stuck with one another.

When Manuel finished singing, he pulled me into a quick, chaste kiss. The mayor smiled at us, winked, and then declared, "By the power vested in me by the great state of Oregon, I now pronounce you husbands. You two may kiss your husband."

The crowd, which seemed to include the entire town of Wilcox, applauded. When I pulled back, I smiled at the man who'd completely changed my whole life in such a short period of time. I didn't know it was possible to feel as much love as I did in that moment.

The reception pretty much ate up our entire yard. Our store catered the food with a lamb stew called *birria de borrego*, *carnitas en cazo de cobra*, and enough homemade tortillas to feed a small nation. The family assured me this was all traditional wedding food, not that I was concerned. It was ridiculously delicious, but all I cared about was officially making this family my own.

We danced to the same maríachi band María had found to play at our surprise engagement. Luckily, they were also open to suggestions and played a few more modern songs—all in Spanish, which felt right. I'd become part of this beautiful Mexican American family, after all.

After too much drinking, eating, laughing, and dancing, the brothers gave speeches, and Uncle Henry also had his say.

Before he finished, he called Papá López up, and they lifted wineglasses and toasted to us. "To señores López y Latham—may you live a long and beautiful life full of love and hope."

"And with children," Mamá López yelled, getting chuckles from all gathered.

"Oh, and one more thing from us and Justin's uncles," Papá López said. "You both leave tomorrow morning for Puerto Vallarta. Hope you like to swim!"

My mouth fell open. "But you said we have too much to do," I said, looking over at Manuel, who was blushing and laughing.

"I'm so sorry, mi amor, I was sworn to secrecy. I wanted you to have a wonderful honeymoon and for it to be a surprise."

Happy tears rolled down my cheeks. I had been so disappointed when I thought we wouldn't be able to go on a honeymoon, but María and Carlos had baby José, and Cassie and Martín had their hands full with baby Ana. It just made sense that we wouldn't be able to get away.

"Really? Puerto Vallarta? Just the two of us?"

Manuel smiled and nodded. "Yes, just me and my husband. Did I choose well?"

I nodded and pulled my husband's face to mine. "Sí, mi amor," I said, using the endearment he used for me. "Es muy bien. We both chose well."

Keep reading for an excerpt from
Water Under the Bridge
by Greyson McCoy!

Chapter One

"Ouch, Marisa, stop hitting me."

"Did you not just tell us you wanted to get to know Landon better?" She whacked my arm again.

"Damn, stop. And yes, but he *is* an overthinker. That's why we're not closer to him. First he overthought our asking him to hang out, then he overthought our being friends."

"And you think he's cute, and haven't made a move 'cause you overthought that."

I sighed. "I should've never told you guys."

"You didn't. Your first cousin there forced it out of you," Owen said, pointing to Marisa and laughing.

"Listen, I'm eighteen, have a car, and am on Grindr. I can name at least six guys I could call when I have that need. What I don't need is a relationship. That's something y'all want."

Owen looked at Marisa and sighed. "So, you know Marisa and I...."

I rolled my eyes. "No duh, Owen, I already know. You two have been making goo-goo eyes at each other for the past year. But you know that doesn't mean I need to shackle myself to someone too, right?"

"You need to do more than fuck a bunch of men who are honestly too old for you anyway. You know, all six of those guys could go to jail for screwing around with you."

"Save your breath, Marisa. I didn't even sign up for Grindr until I turned eighteen. Besides, they're all my age or a year older. You make it sound so weird."

"It is weird. Why do you want to randomly fuck men who mean nothing to you?"

I looked at Owen, who was stifling a grin. "I'm so not going to try to explain to you why guys like random hookups. Just think of it as a difference in our natures," I said as I walked in the direction Landon had gone.

"Wait. For real, Jason, you've got a good heart. Don't become one of those nasty men who, you know, fucks anything that moves."

Owen snorted—the ass hat—and I flipped both of them off but didn't stop. I was a typical young guy with a healthy sex drive, but I didn't fuck anything that moved. Just hot, available men who showed mutual interest.

Marisa and Owen began asking me a week ago who in Northport I'd consider getting serious with, and the only person I could think of was Landon.

I thought about Landon a lot. He was so bookish and nerdy, but he had a tight body too. We had swimming classes together last year, and I'd lusted after that body of his more than a few times. Not that I ever told him. Outside of my two best friends, no one at school knew I was gay.

I could sorta tell he was too, but I had already convinced myself I'd never pursue anything until after we graduated. Being out in a rural high school would've been pretty awful, not to mention dealing with my dad. Shit no, that would not be happening. Even now, living with Marisa and my aunt, he would still be a pill if people knew.

As I reached Landon's house, my resolve began to crumble. What if I never saw him after this summer? *Fuck it.* I knocked on the front door.

Landon's mom answered and immediately invited me inside.

"Honey, your friend is here," she called up the stairs, then disappeared into the kitchen.

Landon came to the railing looking confused. His eyebrows shot to his hairline when he saw me.

"Hey," I said, rubbing the back of my neck. "I wanted to say sorry."

Landon stood watching me, then sighed. "Come on up," he said. Then he turned around and went back into his bedroom.

I took the steps two at a time and watched as he plopped down in front of an old TV and began gaming. "Join me," he said. "I just started, so you can play too."

"Landon," his mom called up the stairs. "I'm going to take this over to Mrs. Hughes. I won't be back until late. Your dad's bringing home fried chicken for supper."

"Okay," Landon hollered after pausing his game.

"Oh, and Jason, tell your aunt I'll call her about the community picnic."

"Yes, ma'am," I yelled back. Unlike my sexuality, it felt good that most people knew I was living with Marisa and her mom, my aunt Kathy, now. No more awkward excuses about why I wasn't going home. Besides with my grandparents gone, Aunt Kathy and Marisa were the only real family I had left. It felt right to live with them.

I heard the front door open and close and looked over at Landon, who had his bottom lip caught between his teeth as he resumed playing.

He blushed, when he looked toward me, the cute way he did when he was feeling self-conscious. "I like you," I said, and his blush deepened.

"Yeah, Marisa said. I still think—"

Before he could go on, I leaned over and kissed his lips gently, in a way he could easily pull back if he didn't want to take it that far.

When I broke it and then searched his face, feeling a little unsure if I'd made the right move, he put his fingers to his lips. "Wow."

Then it was my turn to be shocked when he slid his hands around the back of my head and pulled me in for a real kiss. Tongue and all.

I didn't even register he'd maneuvered me to the floor and straddled me until I felt his crotch grinding into mine. "God, you're so hot," I managed to say. That must've shocked him back to reality because he froze mid-thrust.

"Oh shit, wait. I mean, we shouldn't be doing...."

He moved to get off me, but I slid my hands to his hips. "Wait, just a second ago, you were into this. What changed?"

"You and I have known each other for years, and the three of you want to be friends with me now, and my mom and your aunt are doing the community picnic together, and—"

My laugh cut him off, and I released my grip. "All of that was true before you stuck your tongue down my throat," I said as he slid to the floor and I turned onto my side to face him. "Geez, you really *do* overthink everything."

I could see that last comment irritated him, so I leaned over and kissed him again. When Landon whimpered, I took that as my cue to drape a leg over his hip and pick up where he'd left off. "Mmm, no fair," he said between kisses.

I licked the shell of his ear, then sucked on his earlobe. "Stop thinking. Just enjoy," I said as I began to pull his shirt off.

I wanted Landon Carter, and had for a long time. Now we had a house to ourselves and he was showing me he wanted me every bit as much as I did him. I'd be damned if I was going to stop. He was perfectly capable of stopping if he wanted.

As he lay naked under me, I let my fingers explore his sexy, lean swimmer's build before I retraced every inch with my tongue. Landon squirmed under the attention, which sent a thrill through me.

I was affecting Landon as much as he was me, and I relished the feeling. If I hadn't been so wrapped up in him and this moment, I might've been the one to overthink what all that meant.

SCAN THE QR CODE BELOW TO PREORDER!

GREYSON MCCOY loves to travel. After years of being tied down to a life of kids, work, running a small farm, and all things domestic, he and his husband have taken full advantage of their empty nest to travel the world.

The joy of writing came to Greyson late in life. While completing his master's degree, he found himself fighting between desperately wanting to write fiction and finishing the homework and papers he'd been assigned.

After his master's was finished, Greyson decided to shirk his life of responsibility and pursue his dream of writing full time. His stories reflect many of the locations he and his husband have visited over the years.

Visit Greyson McCoy on his website at www.GreysonMcCoy.gay (his husband assures him that's a real domain extension) and sign up for his newsletter to stay informed of his journey in the world of romance and all things love.

Follow me on BookBub

Bridging Hope

Raising kids and finding love is impossible, isn't it?

GREYSON McCOY

Bridging Hearts: Book One

When workaholic Pierce Simms's sister passes, he suddenly finds himself unemployed, back in the hometown he fled, and raising his niece and nephew. Despite that, he's confident he has things under control—at least until his sister's high-school sweetheart shows up.

With his teaching grant ended, Dalton O'Dell is at loose ends and tight purse strings. Just as the world crashes down on him, he learns his ex-girlfriend has passed and named him guardian of her two young children. Chaos ensues when he and her brother, Pierce, are forced together to raise the toddlers in Pierce's family farmhouse.

Nestled in the enchanting beauty of the farm, Pierce and Dalton bond over the challenges of co-parenting and their shared grief as unexpected love blossoms. Love might not be enough, however, if they can't learn to bridge the gap between their different worlds and overcome the trauma of their pasts.

SCAN THE QR CODE
BELOW TO ORDER!

BRIDGING HEARTS SERIES · BOOK TWO

Bridging Lives

GREYSON McCOY

Bridging Hearts: Book Two

Cliff Anderson hopes to build on the legacy of his late parents, but that dream seems lost when his California homestead is lost to a wildfire. Devastated, he travels to Oregon to stay with his aunt and uncle on their dairy operation while he makes plans for his future.

College professor Brandon Forest has always yearned for a family and a home of his own. Maybe that's why, despite being busy with his job and his side gig as a fantasy author, he's stayed on as a seasonal worker at the dairy farm. The farm feels so welcoming, and working on their dairy farm might be the next step in building the life he's dreamed of.

Then he meets Cliff.

As Cliff and Brandon confront their own broken pasts, they build a connection that runs deep. Laughter and shared experiences prove to be strong medicine for the wounds life has inflicted on them.

Cliff hasn't let go of his past or the hopes he had for the farm in California. Will his future burn down as he holds on to lost hopes, or can he blaze a new path with Brandon?

SCAN THE QR CODE BELOW TO ORDER!

Mending
Bridges

GREYSON McCOY

Bridging Hearts: Book Three

Untold stories and unfulfilled dreams. Rhys Healy inherits a house full of both when he leaves the bustling streets of Portland for the serenity of small-town life.

Xander McLeroy is a dynamic force in the world of construction, but life leads him away from that work and back to his roots in Wilcox. Even though he enjoys the comforting world of his past, he expects it to be a lonely place.

True love demands courage and sacrifice. Can Xander and Rhys learn this in time, or will they risk repeating the mistakes of their star-crossed families?

SCAN THE QR CODE
BELOW TO ORDER!

HOMECOMING for BEGINNERS

It's just a house
until you fill it.

ASHLYN KANE

When Ollie Kent arrives on the front steps of the Morris mansion, he's six months out of the military and the brand-new single parent of an eight-year-old cancer survivor. Now they're starting over back in Ollie's hometown, where he's lined up a job as a live-in caregiver for old man Morris.

So it's kind of a downer when a very hungover, mostly naked man about Ollie's age answers the door and tells him old man Morris kicked the bucket.

Tyler Morris left town at sixteen as a pariah. Since then, he's built a good life for himself as an EMT. But even in death, his father has to get in one final screw-you: Ty can either return to his hometown and act as executor of the family fortune, or let it all go to a hate group.

Between an unexpected job offer and unexpected roommates, coming home doesn't go the way Ty expects. But Ollie and Theo bring the cold, lonely mansion to life, and golden-boy Ollie provides good cover for the town's scorn. The only problem is, Ty's falling head over heels for the world's sweetest and most stubbornly independent single dad, and if he wants to keep Ollie around, he'll have to convince him to let Ty help.

SCAN THE QR CODE
BELOW TO ORDER!

Six Places
TO FALL IN LOVE

LEE PINI

Percy de Villiers has it all: wealth, status, and a famous name—until his father's political scandal brings everything crashing down. Struggling with the fallout, Percy retreats to the South African wilderness to focus on his passion, nature photography. But even in the vast beauty of his homeland, he can't escape the weight of his family's disgrace or the loneliness that shadows him.

Rob Hale, a Hawaiian travel writer by way of Atlanta, has spent years idolizing Percy from afar. When an assignment brings him face-to-face with his photography hero, he doesn't expect their connection to spark more than professional admiration. But a chance encounter leads to an unexpected hookup, and the chemistry between them is undeniable.

As Percy grapples with the emotional wreckage left by his father's arrest, and Rob struggles with his own self-doubts, their fling starts to feel like something more. Navigating cultural differences, class divides, and the looming cloud of Percy's family drama, the two men must decide if they can turn their brief romance into something lasting—or if their relationship will fall apart before it ever truly begins.

SCAN THE QR CODE
BELOW TO ORDER!

www.ingramcontent.com/pod-product-compliance
Lightning Source LLC
Chambersburg PA
CBHW070543100726
47907CB00004B/1243